Valley of Maize

Natalie Buckley Rowland

with Laurel Ruggles

George Ohsawa Macrobiotic Foundation
Oroville, California

Illustrations by Natalie Buckley Rowland
Cover Illustration by Natalie Buckley Rowland
Cover Design by Laurel Ruggles and Carl Ferré
Cover Photo by Michael Busselle/Tony Stone Images

First Edition   1998

©copyright 1998 by Natalie Buckley Rowland
Published by the George Ohsawa Macrobiotic Foundation
P.O. Box 426, Oroville, California 95965

Library of Congress Catalog Card Number: 98-65134
ISBN: 0-918860-56-3

Printed in the United States of America

FOREWORD

I have known Natalie Buckley Rowland for several years. She scribed for me during my macrobiotic consultations at the Macrobiotic Center of New York in 1993 and 1994. During that time she assisted me in the contribution of dietary and culinary preparations; sharing her knowledge and experience with clients whenever possible. She also teaches macrobiotic cooking, giving private sessions for special dietary regimens for those who request it throughout the New York area. She is now devising a special grain milk to be used in lieu of the commercially available non-dairy varieties that come in aluminum-lined packages. A healthful alternative, it will be superior to the ones currently available in most health food stores and will be able to be made at home.

The recipes contained in this book are wholesome and creative, following macrobiotic guidelines with a touch of ingenuity. In addition, I have sampled some of her specialties included in the book and appreciate their high-quality ingredients, good taste, and health-giving benefits. Many of her recipes have been tested by the George Ohsawa Macrobiotic Foundation in Oroville, California with very positive results. The presence of her original illustrations and almost anthropological account of the history of grains and cooking, plus her unique recipes and notes make this work an original and valuable contribution to one's bookshelf.

Marc Van Cauwenberghe, M.D.

INTRODUCTION
INTRODUCTION

4 - VALLEY OF MAIZE

A LETTER TO YOU

I came into this world during the 1950's when just about every kid was raised on Kool-Aid, Tootsie Rolls, and Howdy Doody. Even as a child, however, I was drawn to natural foods. At four, I helped my grandmother prepare large dinners, combining raw vegetables and salt in a bowl. My aunt threw away my "salad," thinking it inedible. She didn't know I was making a quick pickle. Neither did I.

At four and a half, I was hospitalized for an unknown illness, probably one of the most extreme situations in my life, considering the medicines, the sterile, antiseptic environment, the endless stream of machines and tests, the alienation and isolation. Although my family was thankful, thinking that the medicines cured me, I soon turned the corner towards a real cure.

A few months before my fifth birthday, I spent the summer in a tiny house in the country with my grandparents and young uncle. I remember a large wooden trunk kept by the side of the house, filled with earth and earthworms for our almost daily fishing trips. My grandfather dug his hands in the earth and pulled out several worms, then requested I do the same, which I did. We took the worms and our fishing poles to the lake and boarded a wooden row boat, proceeding to the middle of the lake. We brought back the catch of the day, which my grandmother cooked, accompanied by fresh vegetables from the market in town. Other days were spent playing "going to market." With seeds, weeds, and grasses that I picked and placed on an old stone wall, my grandmother played the local townslady shopping for fruits and vegetables as I, the street merchant, negotiated prices and wrapped up the purchase. All of this, combined with mild temperate weather, pure air, wild grape vines, natural diet, a cat, and much love, is an indelible memory of an idyllic time. I believe that this was my true healing after the illness.

Time flew fast to the age of six accompanied by Campbell's soup and Romper Room, not to mention Wonder Bread and Bozo. At ten, I enjoyed TV Dinners, Turkish Taffy and Junket Rennet Custard. Unfortunately these were the foods that were readily available, and I graciously accepted, even craved them. Yet, some instinct of another reality was deep in my consciousness. I felt displeased, unsatisfied, and ill from artificial food and embalmed confections. By the age of twelve, I was looking for whole-wheat bread and eating familia, reading ingredients in everything I bought, and going to the neighborhood health food store. But without familial or peer support, not being able to find any groups embracing natural foods, and being very young and needing acceptance from peers, what I put into my physical body still did not change.

Having developed arthritis by fourteen, I took the sixteen aspirin a day prescribed for my condition by specialists. Apparently it "cured" me. Yet it also frightened me. Mysteriously recovering one year later at fifteen, I prepared for my adult life as an artist. At sixteen, a brief stint with vegetarianism, which I thought meant eating only cooked lettuce and drinking "health" drinks made from pureed canned fruits, proved unsuccessful.

At age twenty-eight, after ending a long-term relationship with a meat eater, I was left sole heir to the kitchen. I dropped it all and found myself roaming the produce markets and health food stores a good hour daily seeking the best apples and red leaf lettuce. The selections were quickly hauled off to my tiny tenement kitchen, the top floor "Ivory Tower" as it was called. As I worked the ingredients, they became transformed into various vegetarian concoctions without dairy, animal products, sugar, refined flours, chemical additives, or artificial leavenings.

Through years of trial and error, study, research, and evolved eating, I became a "macroneurotic," searching for the real meaning of "macrobiotic," trying to understand the yin-yang theory. This would not have been a problem for one living in the Neolithic era when humans naturally practiced macrobiotics. Reading books by George Ohsawa, Michio Kushi, and Herman Aihara can help you understand macrobiotic principles if you are not one of the lucky ones born with a natural ability to grasp it spontaneously.

Very basically, "yin" represents expansive, upward energy; and "yang" represents contractive, downward energy. Yin and yang are opposites, complementing each other, yet each contains elements of the other and neither could exist without the other. The dietary aspect includes the idea that at least 50 to 60 percent of one's diet should be whole grains (in the form of whole cooked grains, cereals, noodles, bread, etc.), 25 to 30 percent seasonal vegetables and 5 percent soup; supplemented with small amounts of fish and seafood, seasonal fruits, snacks, condiments, desserts, seasonings, and beverages. You are advised to chew everything (including liquids) at least fifty times to maximize digestion and to help produce enzymes in the mouth that aid it; and to be grateful for the food you eat, spiritually blessing it.

Five years ago while journeying the streets of lower Manhattan, the idea of writing a cookbook came to me. The moment was a profoundly meaningful one, for it was as if I became a "cooking missionary," appointed by the universe to write a cookbook. Thus, I set forth on a pilgrimage that began in my mind and continued for a very long time in my kitchen, ending with the writing of this book.

You will not find dairy products, refined grains, refined oils, leavening agents (baking powder, baking soda, yeast), refined salt (the supermarket variety), tropical fruits, tropical vegetables, sugar, honey, jam, jelly, meats, or chemicals used in any of the recipes in this cookbook. You will find the use of whole, unrefined grains and flours, unrefined, expeller-pressed oils, various seeds, fruits and vegetables grown in a temperate climate such as pumpkin and carrot, spring water, miso, tahini, dried fruits, kuzu root, agar-agar, occasional spices, brown-rice syrup, maple syrup, and amazake.

• One for one, whole grains replace the refined grains so often used in common recipes nowadays, so that you get more nutrition, a better-tasting baked product, and the fiber you need in your diet.

- The natural sweeteners—rice syrup, barley malt, amazake—are all made from grains that have undergone a natural chemical reaction, turning their starches into sugars. The body will accept them as complex carbohydrates, allowing them to burn more slowly and provide energy for a longer period of time, as opposed to sugar which burns fast and is a highly refined product.

- The expeller-pressed oils are better too; they are pressed at very low temperatures, retaining the trace elements in the oil, without any chemicals used to extract the oil from the source. Expeller-pressed oils have their own unique flavors, which can be strong.

- Natural thickening agents used here include agar-agar, a seaweed made into bars, flakes, or powder, that produces a gel very much like jello but without the use of pig's feet. Next, kuzu root, a natural thickener for puddings, cakes, and custards, made from a wild vine that grows in the mountains of Japan. Arrowroot powder, from the roots of tropical American plants can be used instead of kuzu root, but kuzu is a higher-quality food with more nutritional and medicinal properties.

- Miso, a fermented paste made from soybeans, sea salt, and a grain such as rice or barley, is used in place of sea salt in some of the recipes and imparts a rich, full-bodied flavor. Miso traditionally is used as a base for soup and has properties similar to yogurt in the intestinal tract, containing naturally good bacteria that aid digestion.

- Sea salt is unrefined salt from the ocean. High in trace minerals and containing no chemicals or other additives, it is a necessity for good health and for alkalinizing the blood. Among the superior-quality sea salts are Lima, Muramoto, and Celtic.

Remember—everything in moderation. Although these ingredients and recipes are the best for you in many ways, I have found that consuming too many baked goods can stuff up and stagnate organs and have an ill-producing rather than a health-giving effect. Balance. That is the key word.

In the pages following, you will be supplied with all the necessary information to be successful in your baking endeavors. In addition, a short history of grains, cooking, leavening, and corn will make you an informed cook and may spark your interest even more in this kind of baking, one of the finest and purest styles existing today.

I would like to thank all the people who made it possible for me to devote time to writing this book, and those who ate the results of the recipes, often providing very interesting and helpful comments. My thanks, also, to Laurel Ruggles for her expertise in editing and her helpful suggestions; and to Carl Ferré for his understanding, patience, and calm spirit. Lastly, I would like to thank the spirit of George Ohsawa, for having given me so much enlightening information about life itself and the theory and practice of food, and for helping me to understand the meaning of yin and yang and the natural order of the universe.

Natalie Buckley Rowland
New York

VALLEY OF MAIZE

MACROBIOTIC BREADS AND MUFFINS
NATURAL TREATS AND MORE
OVER 20 CORNBREAD RECIPES

CONTENTS

12 - VALLEY OF MAIZE

THE SIGNIFICANCE OF GRAIN

To Cook or Not to Cook

Cooking was discovered shortly after the use of fire—about 500,000 years ago in Asia and 1,400,000 years ago in Africa. Fusing food with fire seems to have happened purely by chance. One theory propounds that Neanderthal Man had left a freshly killed animal in an unattended area after a hunt, and a fire accidentally ignited it. The resulting odor stimulated the taste buds and gastric juices flowed.

Cooking produces a chemical reaction that helps to release protein and carbohydrates, increasing the nutritive value of foods, plus helping to break down the fiber. It is said by anthropologists and scientists that eating the communal "catch-of-the-day" in a raw state required long hours of chewing skin, flesh, and marrow (after first cracking the bones and scraping it out), and then entering a digestive system that was not built for it in the first place. Man had neither the time nor the intestines to make this kind of feast practical.

Wild game was also the first food intentionally cooked for advantages of taste and digestion. The method used went something like this: A large hole or pit was dug in the ground. The pit was lined with stones to prevent the food's natural juices from seeping through. Large amounts of water, thought to be transported in animal skin bags, were then poured into the pit. A large campfire was lit to heat other stones, which were then placed in the water, making it boil. The food was added, then more hot stones were placed in the "ground kettle" as needed to keep the water at the right temperature.

Grains formally entered man's diet around 12,000 B.C., when the Ice Age was winding down and the earth's climate was becoming less severe and more tolerable for human beings. Groups of people began settling down in one place in anticipation of harvesting wild grain. This created the first villages in civilization, a change from the primarily nomadic style to a hunting-and-gathering one. People learned to cultivate the wild grains over the next two thousand years. By 7,000 B.C., wheat and barley were highly cultivated in Egypt and the Near East. Four thousand years later, around 3,000 B.C. the world population reached one hundred million. Egypt could now grind its own grain (wheat and barley) and farmers could now produce more food than was needed, so the surplus could be used to feed the laborers who were erecting public buildings and tombs. At this time millet also became a widely cultivated grain since wheat and barley would not grow in certain areas.

It is important to note that grains could not be digested properly when eaten raw, for Homo sapiens does not have a digestive system able to break them down. Cooking was and is a way to break down the raw, indigestible parts of the grain and make it compatible with the human digestive system. But this was not enough, since the grains had to be cleaned and husked first. Some of the husking was done by rubbing the grain between stones, but this crude method produced a cereal that even after cooking was rough on the digestive tract. Toasting the grain, which helped loosen the husk and afterwards enabled the grain to be ground into flour, was discovered and used at this time. With the addition of water, a dough was created that could be pressed flat onto a rock and baked into flatbreads or eaten raw as a cereal or gruel. Grain is often toasted in macrobiotic cookery to add digestibility, shorten cooking time, and give it a more-yang quality and nutty flavor.

Throughout the history of humankind, grain has sustained us as a food source more than all others. This complex carbohydrate can be stored for longer periods of time than dried or preserved meat, fruit, or vegetables. It provides minerals, complete protein, slow-burning energy (the best kind, generally), in addition to having a low fat content—in all, a complete, compact, easily storable food. Organically grown grain can be stored for many years, retaining almost all of its nutritive properties and taste when cooked. This is important in times of famine.

It is the food that, with the addition of water, can keep us alive for the longest time, even if eaten as the primary food.

AN AFFAIR WITH CORN

There is something amazing about corn. I love its taste and the myriad products it can be made into, such as cornmeal, corn flour, corn grits, and corn oil. I love to eat and cook the foods that utilize it as the main ingredient, for example: corn muffins, tortillas, cornflakes, corn griddlecakes, succotash, cornsticks, cornmeal mush, Indian pudding, journeycakes and more.

Corn is a truly American grain and its history includes avid use by the early American settlers and the Native Americans, who were the original people to cultivate it. Corn is also America's most popular grain, with the possible exception of wheat, and there isn't a household that does not have in it something made of corn. There are even garbage bags made from cornstarch and a clear food wrap made from corn oil, which preserves food longer and without the toxic gases usually emitted from commercial wraps.

Forty-seven of the recipes in this book contain corn. Many of them do not use oil as a binder, but use ground seeds—almost always hulled raw sunflower. This follows the Native American tradition of using ground corn, water, and ground sunflower seeds in making cornbread. True to the practice of the Native Americans, no leavening is used, except for a "sour" dough, made by letting ingredients naturally ferment. Perhaps you will sense my strong feeling of gratitude toward them, especially for their spirit of respect for our earth.

Leavening

The ancient Egyptians had sophisticated methods of baking bread including leavening with yeast or sourdough to make it rise. Professional bakers baked loaves of bread in a community oven for the townspeople. Besides its use as food, the bread was used for religious purposes as an offering to the Gods, as well as being one of many items placed in the tomb along with the sarcophagus for the journey into the hereafter.

According to H. E. Jacob in <u>Six Thousand Years of Bread</u>, the bible tells us that the children of Israel departed from Egypt in such haste that they had no time to finish the preparation of their bread in the Egyptian ovens. Religious rituals, including the celebration of Passover, performed by the Jews as offerings forbade the use of leavened bread. The idea, basically, was that anything given to God as an offering must be pure and clean. Yeast, or sourdough, essentially a mold grown on grain from the fermentation of bacteria, was seen as decayed, rotten, unclean, and not fit to offer to God. Other cultures such as the Egyptians and the Arabs considered sourness and fermentation to be elements that support life, as opposed to ones that destroy it. Hence, the Muslim's claim that Mohammed had taught them to make a yogurt-like drink, kefir.

Wheat was the grain commonly used for bread since it responded very well to being raised by yeast. Originally the procedure was to knead the dough thoroughly until elastic and smooth and to let it sit in a bowl loosely covered, allowing the natural wild yeasts in the air to settle on the dough. This could have been discovered by accident as a bowl of kneaded dough was left out, then some time later found to be larger and higher than it was before.

One theory states that ale, used instead of water in the batter, was one of the earliest leavenings. This must have been very effective since ale contains more natural yeasts per volume than wild natural yeasts in the air that just happen to settle on the dough. The Greeks and Italians used flour soaked in grape juice or white wine, kneaded and then set aside until it fermented, or wheat flour made into a kind of porridge and then left to go sour.

To create a superior tasting and infinitely more healthful product, all of the recipes in this cookbook are free of any ingredient to make the baked goods rise. Rising is accomplished naturally during baking, or by letting the batter sit for a few hours lightly covered, as the natural yeasts in the air settle on the dough and populate. In some cases, letting a muffin batter sit for even one half hour will improve the quality of the final product.

Chewing very well is one of the keys to enjoying the taste and getting all of the benefits of the whole grains cooked into the bread, cake, or muffin. With a conventionally baked product that has been pumped up with chemicals, leavening, baking powder, white sugar, and refined flours, you really don't chew well because there is nothing to chew. It just melts in your mouth. When it gets to your stomach it turns into a sponge. Next it gets stuck in your intestines where it has a choice of turning into constipation, stagnation, or gas, or all three. As you chew a whole-grain product, you will appreciate the sweetness of the grain as the enzymes convert the starches into sugars. Every ingredient can be used by the body; every ingredient is in its whole form, as you receive slow-burning energy, increased nutrition, more delicious taste, less fat, and a reason to celebrate.

18 - VALLEY OF MAIZE

A GOOD BAKER. . .

It's not at all how proficient a baker you are or how well you follow directions. Many an individual's dream of becoming an accomplished cook has ended early on because of not choosing good, biologically beneficial ingredients.

When you choose biodynamically or organically grown baking ingredients, you are giving yourself all the vitamins, minerals, and fiber which are naturally in the plant; and you are getting no pesticides. You are assuring yourself of more taste because of the aliveness of the plant grown under one of these methods, especially if it is biodynamically grown, a method which exceeds organic standards. Both these methods improve the quality of the soil, contributing to the well-being of the good earth. It seems to me that when I simply hold a fruit or vegetable raised under one of these two systems, I can feel the energy of the plant vibrate through my hand. Upon taking a bite, I experience the union of human and plant having no beginning or end, continuing on through eternity.

As your body responds to this state-of-the-art, mother-nature food, it can now discern the difference between chemicalized and chemical-free produce. Often as a result of these factors, you may experience a difference in energy levels, sometimes an increase, sometimes a decrease. As the body adapts itself to ingestion and assimilation of the improved food, it can go through some large or small adjustments, sometimes perceptible, sometimes not. At some point, if not immediately, you will definitely reap the benefits of a changed dietary regimen. The quality of life is evident as an effect of the quality of ingredients used; that is, the ingredients used will figure immensely in the outcome.

Most of the ingredients used in these recipes are available in your local natural or health food store. Please try to use organically grown grains, fruits, seeds, vegetables, and oils whenever possible for a superior outcome in quality and taste of your baking. Use expeller-pressed or cold-pressed oils, spring water (or filtered water if spring water is unavailable), and sea salt.

All of the recipes are open to experimentation on your part, so feel free, after mastering a few, to change some of the ingredients to suit your individual need. Baking times may vary depending on where you live and oven temperatures may vary depending on your oven. If you like, you may increase the time that a batter sits in a bowl because doing so can improve the quality of the muffin. For example, with a muffin recipe that says: "Let batter sit for 45 minutes," you might try letting it sit for one to two hours.

Substitute one grain for another if you happen to have leftover grain. If the grain is very mushy, remember to decrease the liquid ingredients slightly to compensate for that. If the grain is very chewy and dry, a bit more liquid will be needed.

Eventually you will reach a point where you instinctively will know when to add a little more liquid or a little more flour to your batter in order to achieve a well-baked, moist, springy product. In some recipes a greater proportion of liquid is required than in others. Generally, when rolled oats are called for as the main "flour" or even as half of the main "flour," the batter should contain more liquid, since oats will absorb a lot during the baking process. Some batters will appear very stiff, but because of certain ingredients such as pureed carrots or apples, will need to be so in order that the end product is not mushy.

If you are experimenting with sweeteners, do not use rice syrup as a primary sweetener if you are substituting it for another sweetener. It almost always produces an uncooked, mushy texture, especially when you are baking without leavening.

Don't be frustrated if your first and second attempts seem to be failures, it can take a few tries before you get the results you want. But if you follow the recipe exactly as it is written, remembering to preheat the oven and bake the item for the exact length of time suggested, you will probably meet with success on your first try. In any case, may the good baking spirits guide you to unlimited culinary bliss!

MUFFIN YOGA

Try this: Buy a corn muffin in your local bakery or supermarket. Set it aside in a safe place temporarily. Now make and bake your own corn muffin using all organic ingredients according to one of the muffin recipes in this book. Let it cool. Now take out the bakery muffin, place it next to yours, inhale slowly then exhale slowly. Repeat two times with eyes closed. Open your eyes. Look at the muffins. Are there any visual differences between the two? Now touch both muffins, press the tops down gently. Are they the same? Pick them up. Take a deep breath and smell. Which one is seducing you to eat it? Which one makes you stop in your tracks, enraptured in the deja vu of your Grandmother's kitchen? Ponder this: Take a bite of one. Chew well, at least fifty times. Repeat with the other muffin. Which one do you feel is more compatible with you? Which one makes you feel like you are doing something good for you? How do your teeth feel? Do you hear yourself saying: "This is how muffins should be?" Which one are you saying it to? Could you also be thinking: "This is different, I have to get used to it, but I know that it is right?" And there it is. Maybe your body is in harmony with the high-quality organic ingredients used in making that muffin. If it's the bakery muffin that feels instinctively right for you, chances are your system is numb from years of eating preserved, sugared, and chemicalized foods and you especially need to reward yourself with biologically beneficial ingredients, starting right now.

More Secrets of the Trade

I have found that some of the best vessels for baking breads, cakes, muffins, etc. are made of stainless steel, preferably heavy gauge. Even better if you can acquire it is ceramic or glass. Cast iron is also a good choice if you can persist with keeping the apparatus well seasoned and free of rust. Most good stores will have stainless steel muffin, loaf, and cake pans and also glass and ceramic loaf pans.

Aluminum, non-stick coated, or tin baking pans are not the optimum instruments of a good baker. Aluminum actually leaves an aluminum residue on whatever you are baking. A non-stick surface can affect the texture and produce an unevenly baked item, not fully cooking the inside yet scorching the outside. A very lightweight pan cannot bake evenly and will not produce that old-fashioned look and taste you are striving for.

A word about stirring: The best utensil is a wooden rice paddle. It fits so well in the hand, contouring to its natural shape and movement. It also is an excellent scraper for the bottom of the mixing bowl, both as a spatula and when you are stirring natural ingredients to create an even, well-textured consistency. A wooden rice paddle for stirring is all you really need aside from a blender and grater, and most of the time just using your hands and fingers for a stiff batter is sufficient.

If you prefer not to use a blender, it is possible to grind seeds in a suribachi, which is a Japanese clay bowl, unglazed inside. Grinding is done with a wooden pestle, called a surikogi. Both are available from Japanese grocery stores, good natural-food stores, or mail-order suppliers.

Some recipes ask you to cover the baking pan during baking. The purpose of this is to keep the natural moisture in the baked good, which will improve the taste and texture while preventing it from getting too dry. You can experiment with this. I use a large enamel lasagna pan as a cover, avoiding the use of aluminum foil. You can find your own accessory, whatever will fit.

Be sure to preheat the oven in all cases. If not, you will be unhappily surprised with not being able to calculate how long to bake, unless of course you have beginners' luck, or are a very skillful baker.

To store baked goods in the refrigerator I usually wrap them in a brown paper bag rather than plastic. They keep longer and the aerating quality of the paper prevents molds from forming. If the baked good becomes dry after a few days, you can slice it up and steam it to restore moisture; steamed baked goods are easier to digest. If you have leftover bread, you can cube it or slice it thinly and toast it, then add to miso or vegetable soup as croutons, or cook with the soup for the last few minutes for a sort of dumpling.

When preparing food, don't be angry or think hurtful thoughts; the energy may be transferred to the thing you are making. Three vibrations that are good for stirring and mixing are love, gratitude, and wonder. While cakes are baking, be a channel for respect and positiveness, letting these flow through you. Before tasting the first bite, bow your head in thanks.

QUICK BREADS AND SWEET BREADS

Faithful Corn Bread

Professional Corn Bread

John Barleycorn Carrot Bread

Southwest Barleycorn Bread

Simple Polenta Bread

Fancy Corn Bread

Corn Carrot Bread

Right Corn Bread

Corn, Corn, Corn Bread

Zucchini Corn Loaf

Beauty Corn Bread

Southern Corn Bread

Cornucopia Corn Bread

You Won't Believe Your Eyes Corn Bread

Cream of Rice Corn Bread

My Favorite Corn Bread

Loving Corn Bread

My Corn Bread

Korny Corn Bread

Carrot Polenta Bread

Four Grain Loaf

Rye Raisin Loaf

Sesame Raisin Bread

Quinoa Squash Bread

Four Grain Herbed Bread

Millet Bread and Orange Spread

Squash Bread

Corn Bread #2000

Carrot Buckwheat Bread with Sunflower Seeds and Millet

Faithful Corn Bread

2 cups soft-cooked, short-grain brown rice
1 cup apple juice
2 tablespoons mechanically pressed corn, sesame, or rice bran oil
2-1/2 cups cornmeal
1 tablespoon umeboshi vinegar
1 small carrot, finely grated
unhulled sesame seeds, for topping

Heat oven to 350 degrees. Oil and flour a loaf pan.

Place rice in a mixing bowl. Add apple juice and break up rice until there are no lumps. Add oil and mix. Add cornmeal, umeboshi vinegar, and grated carrots. Mix with fingers using a squeezing and kneading action.

Spread evenly in the prepared loaf pan. Sprinkle with sesame seeds. Bake 45 minutes covered, then 45 minutes uncovered. Let cool.

→ Professional Corn Bread ←

1/2 cup sliced carrots
3/4 cup spring water
2 tablespoons mechanically pressed sesame, corn, or canola oil
1/2 teaspoon sea salt
1-1/2 cups cornmeal
3/4 cup cooked brown rice
3/4 cup cooked millet

Good if you have leftover grains

Heat oven to 350 degrees. Oil and flour a loaf pan.

Place carrots, water, oil, and sea salt in a blender. Blend until carrots are grainy and almost dissolved.

In a large bowl, combine cornmeal with blended mixture. Add brown rice and millet slowly, breaking up any lumps, and mixing until evenly distributed.

Pour batter into the prepared loaf pan and bake for 50 to 55 minutes or until done. Let cool one hour before slicing.

John Barleycorn Carrot Bread

1 cup brown-rice flour

1 cup plus 3 tablespoons cornmeal

2 teaspoons mechanically pressed corn, canola, or sesame oil

1 cup cooked barley

1 cup spring water

1/2 teaspoon miso

1 medium carrot, sliced in thin rounds (should measure
1/2 to 2/3 cups)

This bread is also very good if you omit the carrot, use two pinches sea salt and two pinches powdered dulse instead of the miso, and bake for 50 to 55 minutes uncovered.

Heat oven to 350 degrees. Oil and flour a loaf pan.

In a large mixing bowl, combine flour and cornmeal. Add oil and sift through fingers.

In a blender, place barley, water, and miso. Blend until smooth. Add carrots and blend until coarsely grainy. Add blended mixture to flour mixture, using hands to mix.

Spread into the prepared loaf pan, smoothing the top with dampened hands. Bake for 25 minutes covered, then for 25 to 30 minutes uncovered. Let cool 1-1/2 hours.

Southwest Barleycorn Bread

1/2 cup brown-rice flour
1 cup cornmeal
2 pinches sea salt
3/8 cup raw, hulled sunflower seeds, ground in blender or suribachi
3/8 cup raw, unhulled sesame seeds, ground in blender or suribachi
1 cup cooked barley
1 cup spring water

Bread will improve in flavor if you let it sit one hour before baking.

Heat oven to 350 degrees. Oil and flour a loaf pan.

Combine flour, cornmeal, sea salt, and ground seeds in a large bowl. Set aside.

In a blender, combine cooked barley and water until creamy. Add blended mixture to dry mixture using hands to knead and mix. Add 2 to 4 tablespoons more water to lighten batter if desired.

Spread into the prepared loaf pan, evening the top with dampened hands. Bake for 25 minutes covered, then 25 minutes uncovered or until golden.

Simple Polenta Bread

2 cups hot, cooked millet
1 cup cornmeal
2 pinches sea salt
7/8 cup spring water, cold
2 to 3 tablespoons mechanically pressed canola or olive oil

In a large bowl, place hot cooked millet and set aside. In another bowl, place cornmeal and sea salt. Slowly add water, stirring constantly until evenly combined.

Add cornmeal mixture to millet and stir. Add oil, then knead with hands, squeezing through fingers until well combined.

Oil a loaf pan and spread mixture evenly, using dampened hands. Let sit, one or more hours, covered, until ready to bake.

Heat oven to 350 degrees 20 minutes before baking. Bake for 50 minutes covered, then for 13 minutes uncovered to brown top. Let cool before slicing.

Fancy Corn Bread

unhulled sesame seeds
3/4 cup rolled oats
2 cups cornmeal
pinch sea salt
1/4 cup mechanically pressed sesame oil
2 carrots, cut into 1/2-inch rounds
1 apple, peeled, cored, and cut into quarters
1/2 cup apple juice or spring water
3 tablespoons tahini
2 tablespoons umeboshi vinegar
1-1/4 cups hot, cooked millet

Heat oven to 350 degrees. Oil a loaf pan and sprinkle with sesame seeds. Shake pan and turn upside down to release excess seeds.

Place oats in blender and grind until a flourlike consistency. In a large bowl, combine oats with cornmeal, sea salt, and oil. Mix until oil is evenly distributed.

Place carrots, apple, and apple juice or water in blender and blend until a coarse liquid consistency. (Or leave carrots and apple whole and grate them finely by hand, then add apple juice or water.)

Add carrot mixture to oats mixture. Add tahini, umeboshi vinegar, and millet. Stir until smooth and there are no lumps. Batter should be moist and loose, almost a dough consistency. Add a few tablespoons of water if too dry.

Spread evenly into the prepared loaf pan. Dampen hands to press firmly on top to create an even surface. Bake for 50 to 60 minutes covered, then for 10 minutes uncovered.

Corn Carrot-Bread

2 cups cornmeal
2 cups rolled oats
2 pinches sea salt
4 tablespoons mechanically pressed corn or flaxseed oil
3 cups spring water
2 medium carrots, scraped, and finely grated
sesame seeds, hulled or unhulled

Heat oven to 350 degrees. Oil a loaf pan.

Place cornmeal, rolled oats, and sea salt in a large bowl. Add oil, crumbling the mixture between your fingers until evenly distributed. Slowly add water, stirring with a rice paddle until smooth-textured. Fold in carrots.

Sprinkle the bottom of the loaf pan with sesame seeds. Spread batter evenly in the pan, patting top with dampened palms to even out top. Bake covered for 1 hour then for about 20 to 30 minutes uncovered until golden. Let cool.

RIGHT CORN BREAD

1/2 cup sliced carrots
1-1/2 cups spring water
1 teaspoon mechanically pressed oil
2 cups cornmeal
1 cup spelt flour or whole-wheat flour
1/2 cup leftover cooked grain
1-1/2 teaspoons miso, diluted in 1 tablespoon water
1/4 cup lightly toasted sunflower seeds

Place carrots, spring water, and oil in a blender and blend until pureed.

Place cornmeal in a pot and add the blended mixture, stirring until no lumps remain. Cook, stirring constantly, until mixture starts to simmer, about 2 minutes. Remove from heat and let cool.

Place spelt flour in a large bowl. Slowly add cooked mixture, stirring well. Add leftover cooked grain and stir until no lumps remain. Add diluted miso and fold in sunflower seeds. Add a little water (up to 1/4 cup) if necessary, to make a thick batter.

Pour into an oiled loaf pan and let sit four hours covered with a towel. Heat oven to 350 degrees about 20 minutes before baking. Bake for 50 minutes. Let cool.

Corn, Corn, Corn Bread

1-3/4 cups fresh corn (about 3 ears)

1-1/2 cups water

3/4 cup brown-rice flour

2 cups cornmeal

pinch sea salt

1/8 cup mechanically pressed corn or sesame oil

3 tablespoons sesame tahini

1/2 cup spring water

3 tablespoons umeboshi vinegar

2 carrots, finely grated

You could sprinkle the bottom of the loaf pan with unhulled sesame seeds if you want, then spread batter on top.

Cut corn off ears and simmer for 5 minutes in 1-1/2 cups of water. Remove from heat and set aside.

Heat oven to 350 degrees. Oil a loaf pan.

Combine rice flour, cornmeal, and sea salt. Add oil and mix until crumbly and evenly distributed.

In a small bowl combine tahini, 1/2 cup water, umeboshi vinegar, and carrots. Add this mixture to the flour mixture, and stir well.

Drain water from corn and reserve. Add about 1/2 cup of the water to the mixture. Fold in the corn and mix well. Add a few more tablespoons of the corn water if too dry.

Spread batter evenly in the oiled loaf pan with dampened hands. Bake covered for 70 minutes.

Zucchini Corn Loaf

1/4 cup millet
1/2 cup spring water
1/4 cup rice syrup or maple syrup
1/3 cup sunflower seeds
1/2 cup spring water
3/4 teaspoon sea salt
1/2 teaspoon non-irradiated cinnamon
1/2 teaspoon non-irradiated nutmeg
1 cup cornmeal
1 teaspoon mechanically pressed oil
2 cups finely grated zucchini (do not drain off excess water)

Very moist!

Cook millet: Place millet, 1/2 cup spring water, and rice syrup or maple syrup in a saucepan. Simmer covered 25 to 30 minutes.

Heat oven to 350 degrees. Oil a loaf pan.

Blend sunflower seeds, 1/2 cup spring water, sea salt, and spices in a blender until all seeds are coarsely ground. Place cornmeal in a bowl and add blended mixture. Stir well with wooden rice paddle. Add zucchini and mix well. Add oil and mix again. Add cooked millet and stir well.

Place mixture in the prepared loaf pan and bake for 35 minutes covered, then for 20 minutes uncovered. Let cool 2 hours before serving.

Beauty Corn Bread

2 medium carrots, scraped and sliced into 1/4-inch rounds
1/2 cup apple juice
1/4 cup mechanically pressed corn or sesame oil
2-1/2 tablespoons umeboshi vinegar
1 tablespoon sesame tahini
1 cup cooked short-grain brown rice or millet
2 cups organic cornmeal
3/4 cup organic rolled oats, ground in blender

Heat oven to 350 degrees. Oil and flour a loaf pan.

In a blender place carrots, apple juice, oil, umeboshi vinegar, and tahini. Blend until carrots are coarsely grated, then add brown rice or millet. Blend again until combined, a few seconds.

Mix cornmeal and rolled oats in a large bowl. Pour blended mixture slowly into cornmeal mixture and combine. Add 1/8 to 1/4 cup spring water if necessary to make a very thick batter.

Pour into prepared loaf pan and flatten top with dampened hands. Bake for 45 minutes covered, then 25 minutes uncovered. Let cool.

♡ Southern Corn Bread ♡

2 cups cornmeal
1/2 cup quick-cooking rolled oats
1/8 cup mechanically pressed canola or corn oil
1 cup apple juice
1-1/4 cups cooked millet
1-1/2 tablespoons umeboshi vinegar
1/3 to 1/2 cup spring water
1/2 cup unhulled sesame seeds (optional)

Good served with Carrot Puree.

Heat oven to 350 degrees. Oil a loaf pan or a muffin pan.

Place cornmeal and rolled oats in a bowl. Add oil and mix until evenly distributed.

Place apple juice and millet in a blender and blend until smooth and creamy. Add umeboshi vinegar and blend. Add blended mixture to cornmeal mixture alternately with water until consistency is between a dough and a batter.

If desired, sprinkle bottom of oiled pan with sesame seeds. Spread batter in the pan and press down with dampened hands to even the top. Bake loaf covered for 40 minutes at 350 degrees, then uncovered at 425 degrees for 18 to 20 minutes. For muffins, bake covered for 45 minutes at 350 degrees, then uncovered at 425 degrees for 8 to 10 minutes.

For bagels, shape batter into 6 equal balls. Place on an oiled cookie sheet and press down with dampened hands to 1/2-inch thickness. Make a hole in the center of each by pressing down with index finger and making a circular motion. Sprinkle tops with unhulled sesame seeds and press down lightly. Let stand 30 minutes. Bake uncovered at 350 degrees for 30 minutes.

❀Cornucopia Corn Bread❀

2-2/3 cups cornmeal
3/4 cup quick-cooking rolled oats
few pinches sea salt
1/4 cup mechanically pressed canola, corn, or sesame oil
2 medium apples, cored and sliced, skins left on
1 medium carrot, scraped and cut into 1/2-inch rounds
1-1/4 cups spring water
1-1/2 to 1-3/4 cups cooked millet
2 teaspoons umeboshi vinegar
few tablespoons unhulled sesame seeds

Heat oven to 350 degrees. Oil a square cake pan.

Combine cornmeal, rolled oats, and salt in a large mixing bowl. Add oil, rubbing through palms until well blended.

Place apples, carrot, water, cooked millet, and umeboshi vinegar in a blender. Blend until creamy. Add blended mixture to cornmeal mixture. Mix with hands, squeezing through palms until well mixed.

Sprinkle sesame seeds on the bottom of the oiled cake pan. Spread mixture evenly in the pan, patting down with dampened hands. Bake covered for 60 minutes, then uncovered for 15 to 30 minutes. Let cool.

You Won't Believe Your Eyes Corn Bread

3 cups soft-cooked rice
3 cups cornmeal
1/3 to 1/4 teaspoon sea salt
3 tablespoons mechanically pressed canola or sesame oil
1/3 cup coarsely ground peanuts or toasted sunflower seeds

To improve taste quality of bread, let sit with top covered for two to three hours before baking.

Heat oven to 350 degrees. Oil a deep cake pan.

Combine rice and cornmeal in a large bowl. Add salt and oil. Mix well with a wooden rice paddle. Use hands to mix well, too, squeezing batter through fingers until everything is evenly combined.

Spread batter into the prepared cake pan. Use dampened hands to pat top evenly. Sprinkle peanuts, or sunflower seeds on top, pressing into batter. Bake for 35 minutes covered, then uncovered for 25 minutes.

Cream of Rice Corn Bread

1-1/4 cups cooked brown rice
5/8 cup spring water
1-1/4 cups cornmeal
3 tablespoons mechanically pressed canola or sesame oil
pinch sea salt

Place rice and water in a blender and blend until creamy. Place blended mixture in large bowl. Slowly add cornmeal, mixing until well blended. Add salt and mix. Add oil and mix well.

Place in oiled and floured loaf pan. Let sit 60 minutes, covered. Heat oven to 350 degrees 20 minutes before baking. Bake covered for 45 to 50 minutes or until golden. Remove cover and bake for 10 minutes more to brown top.

!MY FAVORITE CORN BREAD!

1-1/2 cups cornmeal
3/4 cup whole-wheat flour
1-1/4 cups spring water
1 cup carrots, scraped and cut in 1/4-inch rounds
1/4 cup raw hulled sunflower seeds
pinch sea salt

Combine cornmeal and whole-wheat flour in a large bowl. Add sea salt and mix gently.

In a blender, place sunflower seeds, carrots, and 1 cup of the water. Blend for 1 minute or until creamy. Add the blended mixture slowly to the flour mixture. Add remaining 1/4 cup water. Mix well using a wooden rice paddle. (Add an extra 1/4 cup water if the batter feels too dry.) Let sit 60 minutes, if time permits.

Heat oven to 350 degrees 20 minutes before baking. Place batter in an oiled and floured loaf pan. Bake covered for 60 minutes, then uncover and bake 10 to 15 minutes more, for a golden top.

Loving Corn Bread

1-1/2 cups cornmeal
3/4 cup ground rolled oats
2 pinches sea salt
1 cup amazake
1/2 cup spring water
2 teaspoons mechanically pressed oil
1/2 cup cooked brown rice

In a large bowl, place cornmeal, ground rolled oats, and sea salt. Mix gently.

In another bowl, place amazake, water, oil, and brown rice. Stir well, breaking up any lumps. Add amazake mixture to cornmeal mixture and combine well, using a wooden rice paddle. Let sit 60 minutes, if time permits.

Heat oven to 350 degrees 20 minutes before baking. Place batter in an oiled and floured loaf pan. Bake covered for 45 minutes, then uncover and bake 15 minutes more.

❀ My Corn Bread ❀

1-1/3 cups yellow cornmeal
1/3 cup brown-rice flour
1 heaping cup carrots, scraped and cut in thin rounds
1-1/2 to 2 teaspoons barley miso
3/4 cup spring water
3/4 cup apple juice
2 tablespoons sesame tahini
1 cup hot cooked yellow or white corn grits, or millet
1/2 to 1/3 cup unhulled sesame seeds

This corn bread tastes so delectable, you could swear that at least one-half cup of oil was used in the baking. Not so. Only two tablespoons of sesame tahini are used, equivalent to only one and one-half tablespoons of pure vegetable oil!

Place cornmeal and flour in a large bowl and stir until combined.

Place carrots, miso, water, apple juice, and tahini in a blender and blend until just pureed. Add the blended mixture to the flour mixture and stir with a wooden rice paddle until combined. Fold in millet or corn grits breaking up any lumps. Mix well with hands, too.

Cover bowl and let sit 60 minutes. Heat oven to 350 degrees 20 minutes before baking. Oil a ceramic or glass square or round casserole dish, or round cake pan. Sprinkle sesame seeds generously on bottom, then tilt sides until coated, shaking off any excess. Pour in batter, and bake 45 minutes or until center looks done.

Korny Corn Bread

2 ears corn

1-1/2 cups spring water

3-1/2 medium-small carrots, scraped, and cut in 1/4-inch rounds

2 tablespoons sesame tahini

2 tablespoons umeboshi vinegar

2-3/4 cups organic cornmeal

1-1/8 cups ground rolled oats

1/3 teaspoon sea salt

Cut corn kernels off cobs and place kernels in a small saucepan. Add water, level with corn. Simmer covered, 12 to 15 minutes. Remove from heat. Drain corn and set aside. Reserve water and let cool.

In a blender, place carrots, 3/4 cup reserved water, tahini, and umeboshi vinegar. Blend until carrots are grainy.

In a large bowl, place cornmeal, oats, and sea salt. Add blended mixture to cornmeal mixture, kneading with dampened hands until crumbly. Add remaining 3/4 cup reserved water and continue to mix with hands. Add corn to batter and stir well with rice paddle. Let sit 1/2 hour while oven heats.

Heat oven to 350 degrees. Oil and flour a square cake pan. Spread batter evenly in pan. Cover and bake for 50 minutes. Let cool 1 hour.

◎ Carrot Polenta Bread ◎

1 cup sliced carrots

1/2 cup spring water

2 tablespoons sesame tahini

1 tablespoon umeboshi vinegar

1 cup cooked millet

1-1/2 generous cups cornmeal

*If you have time,
let batter sit 30 minutes in a
loaf pan before baking.*

Heat oven to 350 degrees. Oil and flour a loaf pan.

Place carrots, water, tahini, and umeboshi vinegar in a blender. Blend until carrots are all grated and mixture is grainy. Work in millet and blend briefly until lumps are gone.

Place cornmeal in a large bowl. Slowly add blended mixture, working it in with dampened hands. Knead with hands for 60 seconds or until smooth, like the consistency of almond paste.

Place batter in prepared loaf pan and pat top down with dampened hands. Bake covered for 30 minutes, then 20 minutes uncovered.

Four Grain Loaf

1-1/2 cups whole-wheat flour
1 cup millet flour
1/2 cup brown-rice flour
1/2 cup cornmeal
pinch sea salt
1/4 cup mechanically pressed corn oil
1-1/4 cups spring water
1/2 cup cooked millet or brown rice
sesame seeds, unhulled, optional

Heat oven to 350 degrees. Oil and flour a loaf pan.

Mix flours and cornmeal in a large bowl. Add oil, mixing well with hands in a rubbing motion between fingers.

Combine water with cooked millet or rice, then add to flour mixture. Knead well for at least 5 minutes.

Place in prepared loaf pan and even the top with dampened hands. Sprinkle top lightly with sesame seeds if desired. Bake covered for 30 minutes, then for 60 minutes uncovered.

Rye Raisin Loaf

1/2 cup short-grain brown rice
2-1/2 cups spring water
pinch sea salt
6 to 8 cups rye flour
1/2 teaspoon sea salt
1 teaspoon non-irradiated cinnamon
6 tablespoons mechanically pressed sesame oil
1/2 cup monnukah raisins

*Let cool at least one hour
before serving.*

Simmer rice with water and salt for 1-1/2 hours, or pressure cook for 50 minutes. Keep rice hot.

Combine rye flour, sea salt, cinnamon. Add oil, sifting and rubbing through fingers until evenly distributed. Add 3 cups of the cooked rice and knead until the consistency is dough-like. Place on a floured board and knead, adding more flour if necessary. Knead 400 times or until a stiff dough is formed. Add raisins and knead 60 times more, or until raisins are evenly distributed. Form into a round loaf shape and place on an oiled baking dish. Cover with a damp towel and leave in a warm place for 12 hours, moistening towel once in a while.

Heat oven to 275 degrees 15 minutes before baking. Bake for 35 minutes at 275 degrees, then for 70 minutes at 350 degrees.

Sesame Raisin Loaf

1-1/2 to 2 cups spring water
3/4 cup raisins
1 cup oat flour
1 cup millet flour
1-1/4 cups rolled oats
1/2 cup ground sunflower seeds
3/4 cup ground unhulled sesame seeds
pinch sea salt

To make oat flour,
grind rolled oats in a blender

Heat oven to 325 degrees. Oil and flour a cake pan.

Bring water to boil in a pot with raisins. Remove from heat. Drain raisins and set aside. Reserve water and let cool.

In a large bowl, combine oat flour, millet flour, rolled oats, ground sunflower seeds, ground sesame seeds, and sea salt. Add enough of the reserved water to dry ingredients to make a thick batter. Fold in raisins.

Pour into prepared cake pan and bake for 1 hour and 15 minutes, or until firm and well baked. Let cool.

Quinoa Squash Bread

1 cup cooked squash
1 medium apple, cored and unpeeled, cubed
1-1/4 cups cooked quinoa
1-1/4 cups quick-cooking rolled oats
1 teaspoon non-irradiated cinnamon
1/2 teaspoon non-irradiated ginger
2-1/2 tablespoons sesame tahini
1/2 cup rice syrup or 1/3 cup maple syrup
pinch sea salt
few tablespoons raw pumpkin seeds

Heat oven to 350 degrees. Oil a loaf pan.

Place squash, apple, tahini, and rice syrup in a blender. Blend until smooth. Set aside.

In a large bowl combine cooked quinoa, rolled oats, cinnamon, ginger, and sea salt. Stir briefly, then add blended squash mixture. Mix with dampened hands until even textured and well combined.

Spread pumpkin seeds on bottom of prepared loaf pan. Add batter, patting top down evenly with dampened hands. Bake for 50 minutes covered, then remove cover and bake for 20 to 25 minutes.

Four Grain Herbed Bread

2-1/2 cups whole-wheat flour

1 cup cornmeal

1 cup brown-rice flour

1 teaspoon sea salt

6 tablespoons mechanically pressed oil

2 cups leftover cooked grain

2-1/2 to 3 cups spring water

1 cup toasted unhulled sesame seeds

2 teaspoons ground dried sage or dill

Instead of sea salt, try two teaspoons light miso, diluted in two tablespoons water.

Heat oven to 325 degrees. Oil 2 loaf pans.

Place flours and cornmeal in a large mixing bowl. Add salt, if desired, and stir. Add oil and rub through hands until evenly distributed.

In a separate bowl, add cooked grain to water, breaking up grains until combined (or whiz water and cooked grain in blender until creamy). If not using salt, add diluted miso to grain and water mixture. Add grain mixture to flour mixture. Stir well. Add sesame seeds and sage or dill, mixing again until evenly distributed.

Pour batter into prepared loaf pans. Bake for 45 minutes at 325 degrees and then for 25 minutes at 350 degrees or until golden.

Millet Bread and Orange Spread

2 cups cooked millet
1 cup cornmeal
few pinches sea salt
3 tablespoons mechanically pressed corn or canola oil
5 to 10 tablespoons spring water, if needed

Orange Spread:
2 tablespoons tahini
2 tablespoons fresh orange juice
1/2 to 3/4 teaspoon barley miso

Bring millet to room temperature. Add cornmeal, mixing through hands and fingers. Add salt, then oil. Add water, if needed to obtain a spreadable consistency. Continue to mix with hands in a kneading motion.

Spread batter into a well-oiled loaf pan. Pat top with dampened hands to even out. Let sit 1 hour, covered, before baking. Heat oven to 350 degrees 20 minutes before baking. Bake for 45 minutes covered, then uncovered for 5 more minutes. Let cool before slicing.

To make Orange Spread: Puree tahini, orange juice, and miso in a suribachi. Spread on slices of bread just before serving.

SQUASH BREAD

1-1/4 cups brown-rice flour

1 teaspoon mechanically pressed oil

3/4 teaspoon sea salt

1/3 teaspoon non-irradiated allspice

1 teaspoon non-irradiated cinnamon

1/2 cup coarsely ground sunflower seeds

2 cups mashed, cooked butternut or acorn squash, with or without
   skins, or, cooked, peeled baked sweet potatoes

5 tablespoons maple syrup or barley malt

5/8 cup cooked millet or cooked cracked wheat

1/2 cup soaked, plumped raisins, optional

*When cooking squash
for this recipe, cook in apple juice
for a sweeter bread.*

Heat oven to 350 degrees. Oil a loaf pan.

Place flour in large bowl. Add oil, rubbing through hands. Add sea salt, spices, and ground seeds; mix. Add mashed squash or sweet potatoes and sweetener. Fold in cooked grains and raisins.

Place in prepared loaf pan and even out top with dampened hands. Bake 45 minutes.

◎ Corn Bread # 2000 ◎

1 cup cornmeal
1 cup rolled oats, ground in blender
1/4 cup raw, hulled sunflower seeds, ground
1/2 teaspoon sea salt
1-1/2 cups apple juice
2 tablespoons mechanically pressed oil
1/2 cup cooked millet

*For best results,
roast cornmeal in a
cast iron pan.*

Heat oven to 375 degrees. Oil a 6-muffin pan.

Dry-roast cornmeal in a frying pan until aromatic. Pour into a large bowl and add ground oats, ground seeds, and sea salt. Stir. Add apple juice gradually, stirring after each addition. Add oil. Stir. Add cooked millet, breaking up any lumps. Combine until batter is even.

Spoon into prepared muffin tin and bake 15 minutes at 375 degrees, then 30 minutes at 350 degrees. Let cool.

Carrot Buckwheat Bread with Sunflower Seeds and Millet

1/3 cup plus 1 handful raw, hulled sunflower seeds

1-1/4 cups apple juice

1/2 teaspoon non-irradiated cinnamon

1/3 teaspoon non-irradiated nutmeg

1/4 teaspoon sea salt

2 teaspoons umeboshi vinegar

1-2/3 cups brown-rice flour

1/2 cup buckwheat flour

7/8 cup cooked millet

2-1/2 cups coarsely grated carrots

Heat oven to 350 degrees. Oil and flour a loaf pan.

Place 1/3 cup sunflower seeds, apple juice, cinnamon, nutmeg, sea salt, and vinegar in a blender. Blend until seeds are coarsely ground.

Place flours in a large mixing bowl and stir briefly. Add blended mixture to flour mixture. Stir until a dough-like consistency is reached. Add 2 to 3 additional tablespoons apple juice, if necessary, and stir again. Add cooked millet, mixing and kneading batter. Add grated carrots and the handful of unblended sunflower seeds. Mix thoughly.

Spread evenly into the prepared loaf pan. Bake 50 minutes covered. Remove cover and bake 30 minutes more or until done. Let cool 2-1/2 hours before slicing.

MUFFINS

Seed and Fruit Indian Corn Muffins

Beauty Corn Muffins

Millet Corn Raisin Muffins

Amazake Miso Muffins

Blueberry Corn Muffins

Millet Nut Muffins

Triple Rice Bran Muffins

Corn Raisin Muffins

Millet Carrot Muffins

Millet Corn Muffins

Buckwheat Muffins

Three Grain Breakfast Muffins

Lemon Sunflower Corn Muffins

Quinoa Corn Muffins with Raisins

Three Grain Apple Muffins

Lima Millet Muffins

Cranbran Muffins

Rich Corn Bread Muffins

Apple Pumpkin Corn Muffins

Apple Oat Muffins

Hi-Fiber Apple Bran Muffins

Carrot Raisin Bran Muffins

Apple Amazake Corn Muffins

Rutabaga Corn Muffins

Cardamom Breakfast Meal Muffins

Yin Yang Muffins

Muffins

All these recipes will make at least six large muffins, using standard muffin pans with three-inch cups, and filling pans to the top since there is little rising. Any leftover batter can be used to make an extra muffin in an oiled ovenproof coffee mug or custard cup. If you use a twelve-muffin pan and fill eight or ten of the muffin cups, pour an inch of water in each empty cup before baking to prevent warping the pan. If the muffin cups are filled only half or two-thirds full, twelve muffins could be made, but they will be small since unleavened batter will not rise very much. I like big muffins and the idea of having enough batter left over for one extra gigantic muffin.

Seed and Fruit Indian Corn Muffins

1-1/2 cups chopped apples, unpeeled
1/2 cup raw hulled pumpkin seeds
2 tablespoons maple syrup
3/4 teaspoon sea salt
3/4 teaspoon non-irradiated cinnamon
1/2 teaspoon non-irradiated nutmeg
1/3 teaspoon non-irradiated allspice
1/2 cup spring water
1 cup cornmeal
2/3 cup cooked millet
2 teaspoons mechanically pressed corn,
    canola, sesame, or flaxseed oil

If you can't find organic apples, peel them.

Place apples, pumpkin seeds, maple syrup, sea salt, spices, and water in a blender. Blend until a coarse consistency.

Place cornmeal in a large bowl. Add blended mixture to cornmeal. Add millet, breaking up any lumps. Add oil and stir again.

Oil a muffin pan (this recipe makes more than 6 muffins). Place batter in the muffin pan and let it sit 30 minutes while heating oven to 350 degrees. Bake 40 to 45 minutes.

Beauty Corn Muffins

2 cups cornmeal
3/4 cup rolled oats, ground
pinch sea salt
1-1/2 carrots, scraped, ends cut off, sliced
3/4 cup apple juice
1 cup soft cooked millet
3/8 cup mechanically pressed safflower oil or corn oil
1-1/2 teaspoons umeboshi vinegar
2 teaspoons sesame tahini

Heat oven to 350 degrees. Oil and flour a muffin pan (this recipe makes more than 6 muffins).

Place cornmeal, ground rolled oats, and sea salt in a large mixing bowl.

Place carrots, 1/2 cup apple juice, millet, oil, umeboshi vinegar, and tahini into blender. Blend until coarsely blended. Add blended mixture to flour mixture, slowly mixing with a wooden spoon. Add millet and knead mixture through hands to mix if necessary. Add remaining 1/4 cup of apple juice and mix well.

With a wooden spoon, spoon and spread batter into muffin cups. Bake for 30 minutes covered, then for 30 minutes uncovered.

Millet Corn Raisin Muffins

1/2 cup spring water
1/2 cup monnukah raisins
1 cup millet flour
1/4 cup cornmeal
pinch sea salt
dash non-irradiated cinnamon, optional
2 tablespoons mechanically pressed corn or sesame oil
1 apple, cored and sliced
1-1/4 cups quick-cooking rolled oats
handful raw sunflower seeds, optional

Heat oven to 350 degrees. Oil a 6-muffin pan.

In a saucepan, bring water and raisins to a boil. Simmer 30 seconds. Remove from heat and let stand 10 minutes. Drain raisins and set aside. Reserve water.

Combine flour and cornmeal in a large bowl. Add sea salt, and cinnamon if desired.

Drain raisins and set aside, saving the water. Place water in a blender with oil and apple. Blend until coarsely grated. Combine blended mixture gradually with flour mixture to make a batter. Add rolled oats and mix well. Fold in raisins, and sunflower seeds if desired.

Spoon the batter into the muffin cups, filling them to the top. Bake covered at 350 degrees for 30 minutes, then at 400 degrees uncovered for 20 minutes or until done. Let cool before removing from muffin cups.

Amazake Miso Muffins

1-1/2 cups millet flour
1/2 cup rolled oats
1/2 cup brown-rice flour
pinch sea salt
1 tablespoon barley miso
1 cup apple juice
4 tablespoons mechanically pressed safflower, sesame, or corn oil
1/8 cup plain amazake
3/4 cup soft-cooked brown rice or millet
1/4 cup ground raw sunflower seeds

Heat oven to 350 degrees. Oil a 6-muffin pan.

Combine millet flour, rolled oats, brown-rice flour, and sea salt in a large bowl.

Dilute the miso with 3 tablespoons of the apple juice. In a blender place the diluted miso, remaining apple juice, oil, amazake, brown rice or millet, and ground sunflower seeds. Blend for a few seconds until even-textured. Gradually add the blended mixture to the flour mixture, mixing with a wooden spoon.

Spoon batter into the well-oiled muffin cups. Bake for 30 minutes covered, then for 15 to 20 minutes uncovered. Let cool before removing from muffin pan.

Blueberry Corn Muffins

1-1/2 cups cornmeal
1 cup quick-cooking rolled oats
3/4 cup apple juice
1 cup plain amazake
3 tablespoons mechanically pressed corn oil
1 teaspoon barley miso
3/4 cup blueberries

Grind regular rolled oats in a blender if you don't have the quick-cooking kind.

Heat oven to 350 degrees. Oil a muffin pan (this recipe makes more than 6 muffins).

Place cornmeal and rolled oats in a large mixing bowl. Add oil and mix very well, rubbing through hands.

Dilute miso in a few tablespoons of the amazake, in a suribachi. Place diluted miso, remaining amazake, and apple juice in a blender and blend for a few seconds. Add blended mixture to flour mixture and combine until well distributed and even-textured. Fold in blueberries.

Place batter in well-oiled muffin cups. Bake covered for 30 minutes at 350 degrees, then for 15 minutes at 400 degrees uncovered. Let cool before removing from muffin pan.

Millet Nut Muffins

1-1/2 cups rolled oats
1-1/2 cups millet flour
pinch sea salt
1/4 cup mechanically pressed safflower or rice bran oil
1-1/4 cups apple juice
3 small apples, finely chopped or coarsely grated, skins on
1/3 teaspoon non-irradiated cinnamon
1/3 to 1/2 cup coarsely chopped almonds or pecans

Fill muffin cups two-thirds full since these muffins rise slightly when baked.

Heat oven to 350 degrees. Oil a muffin pan (this recipe makes 10 regular-sized muffins).

Combine rolled oats and millet flour in a bowl. Add sea salt. Add oil and work through hands until evenly distributed.

In a separate bowl, place apple juice, grated apples, and cinnamon. Mix well. Add apple mixture gradually to millet-oat mixture, combining with a wooden rice paddle. Fold in nuts.

Spoon batter into the well-oiled muffin cups. Bake covered for 20 minutes at 350 degrees, then for 20 minutes uncovered at 375 degrees. Let cool.

Triple Rice Bran Muffins

1/3 cup raisins
few tablespoons spring water
1/4 cup raw sunflower seeds
1-5/8 cups apple juice
1-2/3 cups brown-rice flour
1/3 cup rice bran
1/4 teaspoon sea salt
1/2 teaspoon non-irradiated cinnamon
1/2 cup cooked brown rice
1 teaspoon mechanically pressed oil
1-1/2 cups carrots, finely grated

Good things come in threes because they have (1) brown rice flour, (2) brown rice bran, (3) whole cooked brown rice.

Place raisins and a few tablespoons spring water in a pot. Bring to a quick boil, then remove from heat and let sit 5 minutes.

Place sunflower seeds and 1/2 cup of the apple juice in a blender. Blend a few seconds until all seeds are ground. Add 3/4 cup more apple juice and blend again until smooth.

In a large bowl, combine brown-rice flour, rice bran, sea salt, and cinnamon. Gradually add blended mixture to flour mixture, stirring well after each addition. Add remaining apple juice and mix well. Drain raisins and add them to batter. Stir. Add cooked brown rice. Stir. Add oil and stir again. Fold in grated carrots. (If batter is too doughy, you may add up to 2 tablespoons additional apple juice.) Let batter sit uncovered for 45 minutes (or at least 20 minutes if time is limited).

Heat oven to 350 degrees 20 minutes before baking. Oil a muffin pan (this recipe makes more than 6 muffins). Pour batter into well-oiled muffin cups and bake for 45 to 50 minutes. Let cool 1 hour before removing from muffin forms. Use a dull knife and trace around edges to facilitate removal.

Corn Raisin Muffins

1/2 cup monnukah raisins
1 cup spring water
1 teaspoon barley miso
2 tablespoons mechanically pressed corn or rice bran oil
3/4 cup apple juice
3/4 cup cooked brown rice
1-1/2 to 1-3/4 cups cornmeal
1 cup quick-cooking rolled oats

Heat oven to 350 degrees. Oil a muffin pan (this recipe makes more than 6 muffins).

Place raisins in a pot with water. Bring to a boil, remove from heat, and set aside 15 minutes.

Place miso, oil, apple juice, and rice in blender. Blend until creamy.

In a large mixing bowl, combine cornmeal and oats. Add blended mixture to cornmeal mixture and stir until well combined. Drain water from raisins and add to it to the batter, stirring well. Fold in raisins.

Spoon batter into oiled muffin cups. Bake 30 minutes covered at 350 degrees, then 20 to 25 minutes at 375 degrees uncovered.

Millet Carrot Muffins

1/2 cup monnukah raisins
1-1/8 cups spring water
1-1/2 cups millet flour
1-1/2 cups rolled oats
pinch sea salt
1/2 teaspoon non-irradiated cinnamon
2 medium carrots, scraped and sliced
1/4 cup mechanically pressed sesame oil or flaxseed oil
2 handfuls raw sunflower seeds

*For a sweeter muffin,
use apple juice in place
of water.*

Heat oven to 350 degrees. Oil a muffin pan (this recipe will make 10 medium muffins or 6 large plus 1 very large muffin).

Place water and raisins in a small saucepan. Bring to a boil and remove from heat. Cover and set aside.

Drain water from raisins and place water in a blender. Set raisins aside. Add carrots to blender and blend until carrots are coarsely grated. Add oil and blend for a second.

In a large bowl, combine millet flour, rolled oats, salt, and cinnamon. Add drained raisins to dry ingredients and stir well. Add blended mixture and stir very well.

Spoon batter into oiled muffin cups. Bake for 45 to 50 minutes or until golden and done.

Millet Corn Muffins

1-3/4 cups organic cornmeal

1-1/4 cups quick-cooking rolled oats

2 tablespoons mechanically pressed corn or canola oil

1-1/4 cups apple juice

1 teaspoon barley miso, diluted in 1 tablespoon spring water

3/4 cup cooked millet

1/3 to 2/3 cup spring water

For a more nutty, golden muffin, increase oven temperature to 425 degrees for the last 12 minutes of baking.

Heat oven to 350 degrees. Oil a muffin pan (this recipe makes more than 6 muffins).

Place cornmeal and rolled oats into a large bowl and add oil. Use a rubbing motion between the palms of your hands to evenly distribute the ingredients.

In a blender, place apple juice, diluted miso, and millet. Blend until smooth. Slowly add the blended mixture to the cornmeal mixture. Then add water, mixing well with a wooden rice paddle.

Spoon batter into oiled muffin cups. Bake, covered, for 50 minutes. Let cool and remove from muffin pan.

Buckwheat Muffins

1-1/2 cups apple juice
1/3 to 1/2 cup raisins
1-1/4 cups buckwheat flour
1/4 cup brown-rice flour
few pinches sea salt
2 tablespoons mechanically pressed oil
1 teaspoon non-irradiated ground fenugreek
1/2 teaspoon non-irradiated ground cardamom
1 cup sliced carrots
1/4 cup hulled sunflower seeds
1/4 cup cooked brown rice

Bring apple juice to a boil and pour over raisins. Let sit 30 minutes, covered.

Combine flours and sea salt in a large bowl and add oil. Rub through fingers until ingredients are evenly distributed. Add spices, and again rub mixture through fingers.

Drain raisins and set aside. Place apple juice, carrots, and sunflower seeds in a blender and blend until pureed. Add blended mixture to flour mixture and stir well. Add cooked brown rice, breaking up any lumps, then add raisins. Stir briskly. Let sit 1 hour covered.

Heat oven to 350 degrees 20 minutes before baking. Oil a muffin pan very well (this recipe makes more than 6 muffins) and place batter in cups. Bake 40 to 45 minutes. Let cool.

Three Grain Breakfast Muffins

1 cup quick-cooking rolled oats (or coarsely ground regular
    rolled oats)
3/4 cup cornmeal
1/3 cup millet flour
pinch sea salt
1/2 teaspoon non-irradiated cinnamon
1/2 cup monnukah raisins
1 cup spring water
1 apple, cored and sliced
scant 1/4 cup mechanically pressed safflower, corn, or flaxseed oil
handful raw sunflower seeds or pumpkin seeds, roasted if desired

*If desired, hand grate apple:
First cut in half, then grate the cut
sides. Add oil and drained raisin
water and mix well.*

Heat oven to 350 degrees. Oil a muffin pan (this recipe makes more
than 6 muffins).

In a small saucepan place raisins and water. Bring to a boil and remove from heat. Let stand 15 minutes.

Place oats, cornmeal, millet flour, sea salt, and cinnamon in a large
bowl. Mix with a wooden spatula.

Drain water from raisins and set raisins aside. Place water in a
blender with apple and oil. Blend until apple is coarsely grated. Pour
apple mixture into flour mixture and stir until evenly blended. Fold in
raisins and seeds.

Spoon batter into oiled muffin cups. Bake covered for 30 minutes,
then for 10 to 15 minutes uncovered. Let cool.

♡Lemon Sunflower Corn Muffins♡

1 cup quick-cooking rolled oats
1 cup cornmeal
pinch sea salt
2 tablespoons mechanically pressed corn, sesame, or canola oil
1/4 cup ground raw sunflower seeds
1/4 teaspoon non-irradiated cinnamon
1-1/4 cups apple juice
juice of 1 lemon
2 tablespoons whole sunflower seeds

Add a few tablespoons of water if the batter is too dry.

Heat oven to 350 degrees. Oil a 6-muffin pan.

Combine oats, cornmeal, sea salt. Add oil. Mix and rub through the palms of your hands until ingredients are evenly distributed. Add ground sunflower seeds and cinnamon. Mix again.

Combine apple juice and lemon juice. Add to dry ingredients. Fold in whole sunflower seeds.

Place in oiled muffin cups and bake covered for 40 minutes, then for 10 minutes more uncovered.

Quinoa Corn Muffins with Raisins

1/2 cup thompson raisins

1 cup spring water

2 cups cornmeal

1 cup quick-cooking rolled oats

4 tablespoons mechanically pressed canola or corn oil

2 tablespoons raw sunflower seeds, ground in blender

3/4 cup cooked quinoa

1 tablespoon umeboshi vinegar

1 organic apple, unpeeled but cored and sliced

1/2 cup plus 2 tablespoons spring water

For a softer top,
bake covered for the entire
45 minutes.

Heat oven to 350 degrees. Oil a muffin pan (this recipes makes between 6 and 10 muffins.

Place raisins and 1 cup spring water in a small saucepan. Boil for 15 seconds. Let stand.

Place cornmeal and rolled oats in a large mixing bowl and add oil. Stir, then roll and rub through your hands until evenly distributed.

Drain raisins and set aside. Pour water drained from raisins into a blender. Add ground sunflower seeds, cooked quinoa, uneboshi vinegar, and apple. Blend for a few seconds or until smooth. Add blended mixture to cornmeal mixture. Stir well with a wooden rice paddle. Add remaining 1/2 cup plus 2 tablespoons spring water and stir again. Fold in raisins.

Place batter in the well-oiled muffin pan, filling cups to the top. Bake for 30 minutes covered, then for 15 minutes uncovered.

Three Grain Apple Muffins

2-1/4 cups quick-cooking rolled oats
1/2 cup raw millet, ground to a fine powder in blender
1/2 teaspoon non-irradiated cinnamon
pinch sea salt
2 tablespoons mechanically pressed canola or corn oil
3/4 cup cooked short-grain brown rice
1-1/4 cups spring water
3 medium apples, unpeeled, cored and cubed

In a large mixing bowl place oats, ground millet, cinnamon, and sea salt. Add oil and rub mixture between the palms of your hands until evenly blended.

Placed cooked rice and water in a blender and process until creamy. Add cubed apples and blend again until smooth. Pour this mixture into oats mixture and use hands to mix, squeezing and kneading until combined (it takes only a few seconds). Let mixture stand 30 minutes.

Heat oven to 350 degrees 20 minutes before baking. Oil muffin pan; this recipe will make 6 very large muffins or 12 regular muffins. If making very large muffins, fill muffin cups full and round tops; for 12 regular muffins, fill muffin cups 2/3 full. Bake for 45 minutes covered, then for 5 minutes uncovered.

Lima Millet Muffins

2-1/2 cups spring water

2 cups muesli

3 handfuls raisins

2 cups millet flour

1 teaspoon non-irradiated cinnamon

2 pinches sea salt

3 apples, each cut in half

1/2 cup mechanically pressed sesame oil

*Use Lima brand muesli
if available.*

Oil and flour a 12-muffin pan.

Bring water to a boil and remove from heat. Add muesli, raisins, millet flour, cinnamon, and salt. Mix well and set aside.

Grate apples coarsely, cut side down and discard skins. Add oil and apples to granola mixture. Mix well. Spoon batter into prepared muffin pan and let stand 1 hour, covered.

Heat oven to 350 degrees 20 minutes before baking. Bake covered for 50 minutes, then remove cover and bake another 5 to 10 minutes. Let cool.

Cranbran Muffins

1 cup fresh cranberries
1/4 cup spring water
few pinches sea salt
1/3 cup maple syrup, or 1/2 cup barley malt
3/4 cup brown-rice flour
1/4 cup rice bran
1/4 cup coarsely ground raw hulled sunflower seeds
1/2 teaspoon non-irradiated nutmeg
1 teaspoon non-irradiated cinnamon
1 cup cooked cracked wheat

Try whole-wheat couscous in place of cracked wheat.

Heat oven to 350 degrees. Oil a 6-muffin pan.

In a saucepan, place cranberries, water, a pinch of sea salt and maple syrup or barley malt. Simmer covered a few minutes or until all cranberries have popped and have started to "melt." Remove from heat.

Place flour, rice bran, ground seeds, and a pinch of sea salt in a mixing bowl and stir. Add spices and stir again. Drain liquid from cranberries and set cranberries aside. Pour liquid into flour mixture, stirring well. Add cooked grain and stir well. If mixture is too dry, add a slight amount of water to moisten. Fold in cranberries.

Place batter in oiled muffin cups and bake for 40 minutes or until done. Let cool. Use a dull knife around edges of muffin cups to help remove muffins.

Rich Corn Bread Muffins

1-1/3 cups cornmeal
3/4 cup brown-rice flour
1/3 cup raw hulled sunflower seeds
1/2 cup carrots, scraped and sliced
3/4 cup apple juice
3/4 cup spring water
4 teaspoons umeboshi vinegar
2 teaspoons mechanically pressed oil
1/2 cup cooked millet

Heat oven to 350 degrees. Oil a 12-muffin pan.

In a large bowl place cornmeal and flour.

In a blender, place sunflower seeds and carrots. Add apple juice and blend until smooth and creamy. Add water and umeboshi vinegar. Blend a few seconds more. Pour blended mixture onto flour mixture and stir with a wooden rice paddle until well combined. Add millet and stir until evenly distributed. Add oil and stir again.

Fill muffin cups 2/3 full. Bake 35 minutes covered then 15 minutes uncovered. Let cool. Insert a dull knife around edges and sides to facillitate removal of muffins.

Apple Pumpkin Corn Muffins

1 cup cornmeal
1/2 cup quick-cooking rolled oats
2 tablespoons mechanically pressed oil
1/4 cup raw hulled pumpkin seeds
1/2 cup spring water
1/4 teaspoon non-irradiated cinnamon
1/3 teaspoon sea salt
2 cups grated peeled apples
1/2 cup cooked millet

Heat oven to 350 degrees. Oil a muffin pan (this recipe makes more than 6 large muffins or 10 to 12 medium-small muffins).

Place cornmeal and rolled oats in a large bowl. Add oil and mix through hands and fingers.

In a blender, place pumpkin seeds, spring water, cinnamon, and sea salt. Blend until seeds are almost ground, leaving a few seeds whole. Add blended mixture to cornmeal mixture. Stir until dough-like. Fold in grated apples. Add millet, making sure you break up all lumps. Mix well.

Place batter in oiled muffin cups. Bake for 40 to 45 minutes. Let cool.

Apple Oat Muffins

1/4 cup raw hulled sunflower seeds
1 cup quick-cooking rolled oats
1-1/2 cups apple juice
1/2 cup cooked millet
1 cup cornmeal
1/4 teaspoon sea salt
sprinkle non-irradiated cinnamon
2 tablespoons quick-cooking rolled oats
1 large apple, peeled and coarsely grated

Heat oven to 350 degrees. Oil a muffin pan (this recipe makes more than 6 muffins).

Place sunflower seeds, 1 cup of rolled oats, and apple juice in a blender. Blend until smooth and creamy. Add cooked millet. Blend until millet is worked in. Set aside.

In a large bowl, mix cornmeal, sea salt, cinnamon, and 2 tablespoons rolled oats. Stir blended mixture slowly into cornmeal mixture. Fold in apple.

Spoon batter into oiled muffin pan. Bake for 35 minutes covered, then 28 to 30 minutes uncovered. Let cool.

✿Hi-Fiber Apple Bran Muffins✿

1/3 cup raisins
3/4 cup spring water
4 cups diced apples, cored, unpeeled
1 teaspoon non-irradiated cinnamon
1/2 teaspoon non-irradiated nutmeg
1/2 teaspoon sea salt
1/3 cup raw hulled pumpkin seeds
1/2 cup rice bran
3/4 cup rolled oats
1/2 cup brown-rice flour
1 teaspoon mechanically pressed oil

Heat oven to 350 degrees. Oil a 12-muffin pan.

Bring water to a boil. Pour over raisins and soak until raisins are plump. Drain raisins and set aside. Place water in a blender with apples, spices, sea salt, and pumpkin seeds. Blend until a coarse consistency.

In a large bowl, place rice bran, rolled oats, and brown-rice flour. Stir. Add blended mixture to bran mixture. Stir well. Add oil and stir. Fold in raisins.

Place batter in oiled muffin pan. Bake for 50 minutes.

Carrot Raisin Bran Muffins

1 cup spring water
1/2 cup thompson raisins
1 cup brown-rice flour
1/4 cup rice bran
1/2 teaspoon non-irradiated nutmeg
1 teaspoon non-irradiated cinnamon
1/2 teaspoon non-irradiated ground ginger
3/4 teaspoon sea salt
1-2/3 cups sliced carrots
3 tablespoons maple syrup, optional
1/3 cup raw hulled sunflower seeds
1 cup cooked cracked-wheat cereal
2 tablespoons mechanically pressed oil

Also good using cooked bulghur wheat in place of cracked-wheat cereal.

Heat oven to 350 degrees. Oil a 12-muffin pan.

Pour spring water over raisins. Bring to a boil and remove from heat. Cover and set aside.

In a bowl, place brown-rice flour, rice bran, spices, and sea salt.

Drain raisins and set aside. Place drained water in a blender with carrots, maple syrup, if desired, and sunflower seeds. Blend until smooth. Add the blended mixture to flour mixture. Stir. Add cooked cracked wheat and stir well. Add oil and stir. Fold in raisins.

Distribute evenly amongst oiled muffin cups. Bake for 40 minutes uncovered. Let cool.

Apple Amazake Corn Muffins

1-1/4 cups quick-cooking rolled oats
1/4 cup cornmeal, toasted
1/2 teaspoon non-irradiated nutmeg
1/2 teaspoon sea salt
1/3 cup ground sunflower seeds
1-1/8 cups plain amazake
3/4 cup cooked millet
1 tablespoon mechanically pressed oil
2 large apples, peeled and coarsely grated

*Use a dull knife
to trace around edges of muffin
cups to facillitate removal
of muffins.*

Heat oven to 350 degrees. Oil a 6-muffin pan (this recipe makes more than 6 muffins).

In a large bowl, place rolled oats, cornmeal, nutmeg, sea salt, and ground seeds. Stir. Add amazake and stir until combined. Add cooked millet, breaking up any lumps and stir until evenly distributed. Add oil and stir again. Fold in grated apple.

Distribute evenly in the oiled muffin pan, using dampened hands to even tops of muffins. Bake for 45 to 50 minutes. Serve warm.

Rutabaga Corn Muffins

2-1/2 cups cornmeal
3/4 cup oat bran
1/3 pumpkin seeds
1/3 cup maple syrup
few pinches sea salt
2 tablespoons corn, sesame, or flax oil
1-1/2 cups spring water
1 cup loosely packed fresh cooked millet
3/4 cup finely grated rutabaga (yellow turnip)

Heat oven to 350 degrees. Oil a muffin pan (this recipe makes more than 6 muffins).

In a large bowl, place cornmeal and oat bran. Stir until combined.

In a blender, place pumpkin seeds, maple syrup, sea salt, oil, and 1/3 cup of the water. Blend until seeds are ground. Add remainder of water and blend a few more seconds on high speed. Slowly add blended mixture to cornmeal mixture, combining well with a wooden rice paddle. Add cooked millet and mix well. Add grated rutabaga and mix well again.

Fill prepared muffin cups. (There will be enough batter left over for one gigantic muffin, baked in an oiled mug or coffee cup.) Bake exactly 45 minutes and no longer.

✳ Cardamom Breakfast Meal Muffins ✳

3/4 cup brown-rice flour
1/2 cup cornmeal
1/3 to 1/2 teaspoon sea salt
1/2 teaspoon non-irradiated ground cardamom
2 tablespoons mechanically pressed oil
1/3 cup raw hulled sunflower seeds
2/3 cup spring water
2 tablespoons maple syrup
1-1/2 cups apples, peeled, cored, and grated
1 cup cooked millet

Variation: Use cornmeal in place of brown-rice flour and rice bran in place of cornmeal. Add one-fourth teaspoon ground fenugreek along with cardamom.

In a large bowl, combine brown-rice flour, cornmeal, salt, and cardamom. Add oil and rub between fingers until texture is even.

Place sunflower seeds, spring water, and maple syrup in a blender. Blend a few seconds or until seeds are almost ground. Add blended mixture to flour mixture. Stir well until combined. Add grated apples and mix again. Add cooked millet, breaking up any lumps. Use hands and fingers in a kneading motion to combine. Don't be afraid to mix this way. Place a plate on top of bowl and let stand 30 minutes.

Heat oven to 350 degrees 20 minutes before baking. Oil a muffin pan (this recipe makes more than 6 muffins). Place batter in cups, rounding out tops with dampened hands. Bake 45 to 60 minutes. Let cool 1-1/2 hours.

Yin Yang Muffins

2-1/4 cups cooked buckwheat
1/8 teaspoon sea salt
1 cup cornmeal
1/4-1/3 cup water
1 generous tablespoon mechanically pressed sesame or canola oil
1/2 cup thompson raisins

Appropriately called, since buckwheat is most yang cereal and corn most yin.

Heat oven to 350 degrees. Oil and dust with cornmeal a 6-muffin pan.

Place cooked buckwheat into a large bowl and sprinkle sea salt and cornmeal over it. Mix with dampened hands in a kneading motion, squeezing through fingers and palms. Add water and mix. Add oil and mix again. Knead in raisins.

Spoon batter generously into prepared pan, patting down and rounding off tops with dampened hands. (You could let muffins sit 45 minutes to 1 hour in muffin pan before baking for a richer muffin.) Bake for 35 minutes covered, then for 15 minutes uncovered. Let cool at least 1 hour before removing from pan by running a dull knife around edges.

CAKES AND OTHER GOODIES

Dried Fruit Carrot Cake

Carrot Millet Cake

Blue Corn Betty

Fruit and Seed Fruitcake

Indian Harvest Cake

Apricot Hunza Cake

Dried Apple Crisp

Azuki Brownies

Tofu Lemon Cheesecake (Oat Nut Crust)

Carrot Cake

Millet Tea Cake

Polenta Millet Apple Cake

Armenian Apple Cake

Hiker's Carrot Cake

Purest Pumpkin Pie

Halavah Snacks

Almond Carrot Oatmeal Cookies

The Pumpkin Pie Your Mother Never Gave You

(Sunflower Millet Crust)

Depression Cake

Romanian Poppyseed Cake

Dried Fruit Carrot Cake

1 cup apple juice
1/2 to 2/3 cup dried fruit (raisins, apricots, apples, etc.
   or a combination)
1/2 cup ground sunflower seeds
1/2 cup rolled oats
1 cup brown-rice flour, toasted lightly
2 or 3 medium carrots, sliced
1/2 teaspoon non-irradiated nutmeg
1 teaspoon non-irradiated cinnamon
1/3 teaspoon sea salt

Heat oven to 350 degrees. Oil a loaf pan.

Bring apple juice and dried fruit to a boil in a medium pot. Turn down heat and simmer 2 minutes. Remove from heat and let stand covered for 10 to 15 minutes.

Combine sunflower seeds, rolled oats, and toasted flour in a large bowl. Set aside.

Drain apple juice from dried fruit and set fruit aside. Place drained apple juice in a blender with carrots, spices, and sea salt. Blend until a coarse consistency. Add blended mixture to dry mixture. Stir well. Fold in dried fruit.

Place in the oiled loaf pan and even out the top with dampened hands. Bake for 60 minutes. Let cool.

Carrot Millet Cake

1 cup millet flour
1/2 cup oat flour (rolled oats ground in blender)
2 teaspoons non-irradiated cinnamon
1 cup finely ground sunflower seeds
1/2 teaspoon sea salt
2 cups finely grated carrots
1/2 teaspoon umeboshi vinegar
1 cup apple juice
1/2 cup raisins

Instead of grating carrots, you may slice them, then blend with apple juice and umeboshi vinegar in a blender, stopping while the texture is still slightly gritty.

Heat oven to 350 degrees. Oil and flour a loaf pan.

Combine flours, cinnamon, sunflower seeds, and salt in a very large bowl. Mix with a wooden paddle.

In another bowl, combine grated carrots, apple juice, and umeboshi vinegar. Add carrot mixture to dry ingredients and mix with a rice paddle. Fold in raisins.

Spoon batter into the prepared loaf pan. Bake covered for 160 minutes. Remove cover and bake for 30 minutes. Let cool.

Blue Corn Betty

Topping:
- 1 cup blue cornmeal
- 1/4 cup instant rolled oats
- 3/4 cup plain amazake
- 2 teaspoons mechanically pressed oil

Filling:
- 1/3 cup raisins
- 7 medium apples, peeled if desired, and diced
- 1/2 teaspoon non-irradiated cinnamon
- 1 tablespoon kuzu, dissolved in 3 to 4 tablespoons spring water
- 1/4 cup spring water

In a bowl, combine dry ingredients for topping. In another bowl, combine amazake and oil. Gradually add wet ingredients to dry ingredients, in several additions, mixing until smooth after each addition. Cover bowl with a damp cloth and let stand three hours in a warm place.

Heat oven to 350 degrees 20 minutes before baking. Oil a rectangular or a deep round baking pan.

Place diced apples in a large bowl and add raisins. Add diluted kuzu, cinnamon, and water. Mix slightly or until evenly distributed.

Place apple mixture evenly in prepared pan. Spread topping over the apple mixture. If the baking pan is very full, place a cookie sheet under it on the oven rack in case the apple filling bubbles over. Bake 40 to 45 minutes or until top crust is golden around edges. Let cool before serving.

Fruit and Seed Fruitcake

1 cup raisins or chopped dried apricots, or 1/2 cup chopped
dried apricots plus 1/2 cup raisins
2-1/8 cups apple juice
1/2 cup unhulled sesame seeds, ground
1 cup rolled oats, ground to flour
1/2 cup sunflower seeds, ground
1 cup millet flour
2 teaspoons non-irradiated cinnamon

Heat oven to 325 degrees. Oil and flour a cake pan.

Combine raisins and/or apricots, apple juice, and unhulled sesame seeds in a saucepan. Bring to a boil and simmer one minute. Remove from heat. Let stand 10 minutes.

Combine oat flour, ground sunflower seeds, millet flour, and cinnamon in a large bowl. Stir well. Add fruit mixture to dry ingredients gradually. Mix well with a wooden rice paddle. Batter will be very thick.

Transfer the batter to the prepared cake pan. Bake 60 minutes or until done. Let cool several hours before removing from pan.

Indian Harvest Cake

1/2 cup raisins

1/2 cup spring water

1-3/4 cups cooked squash, mashed

4 tablespoons maple syrup

1/2 cup amazake

pinch sea salt

1/4 teaspoon non-irradiated ginger

1/4 teaspoon non-irradiated cinnamon

1-3/4 cups cooked millet

1 cup cornmeal

1 tablespoon mechanically pressed canola, sesame, or corn oil

2/3 cup ground raw, hulled pumpkin seeds

few drops natural soy sauce

Use acorn, buttercup, butternut or hokkaido. Use some of skins if desired.

Place raisins and water in a saucepan. Bring to a boil and remove from heat. Let stand.

In a bowl, combine squash, maple syrup, and amazake. Mix well. Add sea salt and spices. Add millet, stirring until smooth. Add cornmeal and oil. Mix again. Drain raisins and reserve water. Add raisins to mixture. If batter is too stiff, add some of the reserved water.

Oil a loaf pan. Place half of the batter evenly in the pan. Spread ground pumpkin seeds evenly over the batter. Sprinkle with a few drops of soy sauce. Cover with rest of batter. Even the top with dampened hands. Let stand 2 hours. Heat oven to 350 degrees 20 minutes before baking. Bake for 25 minutes covered, then for 40 to 45 minutes uncovered. Let cool.

Apricot Hunza Cake

2 cups spring water
1-1/2 cups organic dried apricots, chopped
1 tablespoon kuzu, dissolved in 3 to 4 tablespoons spring water
1-1/2 cups rolled oats
1-1/2 cups millet flour
pinch sea salt
1 tablespoon non-irradiated ground coriander
1/4 cup mechanically pressed sesame or corn oil
1-1/4 cups spring water

For a sweeter cake, use an equal measure of apple juice in place of the one and one-fourth cups spring water.

Heat oven to 375 degrees. Oil and flour a round cake pan.

Boil the 2 cups water in a saucepan. Remove from heat and add apricots. Cover and let soak 2 hours. Add kuzu and mix. Bring to boil, turn heat to low, and stir constantly until thickened. Remove from heat and let cool while mixing batter.

Combine oats, millet flour, sea salt, and coriander in a bowl. Add oil and stir until evenly distributed. Add 1-1/4 cups water or apple juice and stir well.

Spread apricot mixture evenly in prepared pan. Pour batter on top and spread evenly. Bake for 50 minutes.

Dried Apple Crisp

1/4 lb. organic dried apples
2-1/4 cups spring water
2 teaspoons kuzu, dissolved in 2 tablespoons spring water
1/2 cup raisins
1 teaspoon non-irradiated cinnamon
1/4 teaspoon non-irradiated allspice
1 tablespoon rice syrup

Topping:
1 cup rolled oats
2 tablespoons mechanically pressed sesame or corn oil
1/4 cup whole-wheat flour or rye flour
1 tablespoon rice syrup

Heat oven to 375 degrees. Oil a shallow baking pan.

Soak apples in water for 20 minutes.

Add kuzu to apples and mix well. Add raisins, spices, and rice syrup. Stir until combined. Place in the prepared baking pan.

Place rolled oats in bowl and add oil. Mix well. Add flour and mix well. Add rice syrup and mix again. Sprinkle topping over apple mixture. Cover and bake 25 minutes. Bake 15 minutes more uncovered. Let cool.

Azuki Brownies

2 cups pureed azuki beans (drain liquid from beans first, then puree)
1/2 cup barley malt
1/4 teaspoon sea salt
2 tablespoons kuzu, dissolved in 5 tablespoons spring water

Place azuki beans, barley malt, and salt in a saucepan. Add dissolved kuzu. Stir very well with a rice paddle. Bring to a boil, stirring constantly, and turn down to a simmer, continuing to stir until very thick. Pour into a cake pan and let set. When cool, cut in squares.

Tofu Lemon Cheesecake (Oat Nut Crust)

Oat Nut Crust:

 1 cup rolled oats

 1/2 cup ground almonds

 1/2 cup ground walnuts

 3 tablespoons mechanically pressed sesame or corn oil

 1/4 teaspoon sea salt

 2 tablespoons rice syrup

 1/4 cup water, plus a few more tablespoons if needed

Filling:

 16 oz. firm tofu

 1 tablespoon tahini

 juice of 2 lemons

 1/3 cup plus 1 tablespoon maple syrup

 1 tablespoon mirin

 1 teaspoon grated lemon peel

Heat oven to 350 degrees.

 Gently toast oats, almonds, and walnuts together for a few seconds until aromatic.

 Combine all crust ingredients. Press into a 9-inch pie pan with dampened hands, smoothing out crust. Bake for 10 to 15 minutes. Let cool 10 minutes before adding filling.

 Meanwhile, prepare filling. Drain water from tofu and discard. Cut tofu into cubes. Steam for two minutes. Place all ingredients into a blender and process until smooth. Pour filling into pie crust and bake at 350 degrees for 20 to 25 minutes or until firm.

Carrot Cake

2/3 cup monnukah raisins

3/4 cup water

3 medium unpeeled apples, cored and sliced

1/4 to 1/3 cup mirin or maple syrup

2 teaspoons non-irradiated cinnamon

1 teaspoon non-irradiated ground ginger or 1 teaspoon
fresh ginger juice

1/4 cup mechanically pressed canola or sesame oil

1 cup cooked millet

2 cups quick cooking oats

1 cup whole uncooked millet, ground powder-fine in blender

1/3 cup raw sunflower seeds, ground fine in blender

2 cups medium-finely grated carrots (carrots will be more
visible the less finely they are grated)

It's worth it!
Adapted from the world's oldest
carrot cake recipe.

Heat oven to 350 degrees. Oil a square cake pan.

Place raisins and water in a pot. Bring to boil and remove from heat. Let stand a few minutes.

Drain raisins and set aside. Place water in a blender with apples, mirin, spices, oil, and cooked millet. Blend until smooth and creamy.

In a very large mixing bowl, place rolled oats, millet flour (previously ground in blender), and ground sunflower seeds. Slowly add blended mixture to dry mixture. With dampened hands, squeeze mixture through palms and fingers until evenly combined. Fold in drained raisins. Fold in grated carrots and mix. Batter should be moist but somewhat dense. Add a few additional tablespoons of water if too dry.

Spread into the well-oiled cake pan. Dampen hands well to even out top and spread evenly, then oil hands and pat top of cake. Bake for 45 to 50 minutes, covered. Remove cover and bake 30 to 35 minutes more. Let cool.

Millet Tea Cake

3/8 cup golden raisins
1 cup spring water
1-3/4 cups cooked millet
1-1/3 cups yellow cornmeal
2 pinches sea salt
1/3 teaspoon non-irradiated cinnamon
3 tablespoons mechanically pressed canola oil

Boil water and pour over raisins in a bowl. Immediately pour off water and reserve. Set raisins aside.

Place millet and reserved water in a blender and blend until smooth and creamy. Place blended mixture in a large bowl. Gradually add cornmeal, stirring after each addition. Add salt and cinnamon. Stir. Add oil and stir. Fold in raisins and stir well again.

Oil and generously dust a loaf pan with cornmeal. Spread batter evenly in pan, patting top with dampened hands to even it out. Let stand 2 hours covered. Heat oven to 350 degrees 20 minutes before baking. Bake for 45 minutes covered, then for 10 minutes uncovered. Let cool,

Polenta Millet Apple Cake

1 cup spring water.

1/3 cup golden or thompson raisins

1-1/2 cups cooked millet

1 cup polenta (coarsely ground cornmeal) uncooked

1/3 teaspoon non-irradiated cinnamon

2 pinches sea salt

3 tablespoons mechanically pressed canola or corn oil

2 medium-large apples, cored, peeled, and chopped

Boil water and pour over raisins in a bowl. Immediately pour off water and reserve. Set raisins aside.

Place millet and reserved water in a blender and blend until smooth and creamy. Place in large bowl. Gradually add polenta and stir until well combined. Add cinnamon, salt, and oil. Mix well.

Oil and flour a loaf pan. Spread half of batter evenly in the pan. Place apples evenly on top of the batter. Place raisins evenly on top of apples. Pour rest of batter on top, using dampened hands to spread it evenly. Let stand for 2 to 3 hours, covered. Heat oven to 350 degrees 20 minutes before baking. Bake covered for 50 minutes, then for 10 minutes more uncovered. Let cool.

Armenian Apple Cake

1-1/4 cups brown-rice flour

1 cup rolled oats

1/4 teaspoon sea salt

1 cup spring water

1/3 cup unhulled sesame seeds

1 medium apple, cored and sliced

4 cups ripe, sweet apples, cored, peeled, and coarsely cubed

1/4 teaspoon sea salt

1/3 teaspoon non-irradiated cinnamon

2 tablespoons brown-rice syrup

Heat oven to 350 degrees. Oil a cake pan.

Combine flour, oats, and 1/4 teaspoon sea salt in a large bowl. Set aside.

Combine water, seeds, and sliced apple in a blender. Blend until seeds are ground. Add blended mixture to flour mixture. Mix well.

Place cubed apples in a large bowl. Sprinkle with 1/4 teaspoon sea salt and cinnamon. Mix, then add rice syrup and mix again.

Place apple mixture evenly in prepared cake pan. Spread prepared batter on top evenly. Poke holes all over with a fork. Bake 15 minutes covered, then 35 minutes uncovered. Let cool.

Hiker's Carrot Cake

1-1/2 cups brown-rice flour
1/2 cup ground rolled oats (grind in blender until flour-like)
pinch sea salt
1 teaspoon non-irradiated cinnamon, or 2/3 teaspoon cinnamon
    and 1/3 teaspoon non-irradiated allspice
1 cup finely ground raw sunflower seeds
1 cup plain amazake
1-3/4 cups carrots, peeled and cut into thin rounds
1/2 cup thompson raisins

*You'll be on cloud nine
after & during eating.*

In a large bowl, combine brown-rice flour, oat flour, sea salt, spices, and sunflower seeds until even consistency. Set aside.

Place amazake and carrots in a blender and blend until carrots are coarsely grated and mixture is pulpy. Add blended mixture to the flour mixture. Use hands and fingers to mix thoroughly, forming a thick batter. Add raisins and mix again in this fashion.

Pour mixture into an oiled and floured loaf pan. Even the top by patting with dampened hands. Cover and let set 30 minutes to 1 hour. Heat oven to 350 degrees 20 minutes before baking. Bake covered for 30 minutes, then for 30 minutes more uncovered. Let cool completely before cutting.

Purest Pumpkin Pie

4-1/2 cups buttercup squash, cut in chunks and peeled if waxed
1-1/2 cups spring water
5 tablespoons agar-agar flakes
1/2 cup cooked short-grain brown rice
1/2 cup maple syrup
pinch sea salt
3/4 teaspoon non-irradiated allspice
1-1/2 teaspoons non-irradiated cinnamon
1 baked 9-inch pie crust

If you are not opposed to the pumpkin filling sporting a dark-greenish tinge, then do not discard some or all of the skins. It is healthy to eat the skins. However, if you desire that traditional orange-yellow color, completely discard skins.

Cook squash in spring water until tender. Drain squash and save 1 cup of the cooking water. (Discard remaining cooking water or use for soup stock.) Scoop squash meat off skins, if cooked unpeeled, and discard skins. Set squash aside.

Place the 1 cup of cooking water in a small saucepan. Sprinkle agar-agar flakes on top and let sit 5 minutes. Bring to a boil. Turn heat down and simmer 4 minutes.

Place agar-agar mixture in a blender with rice and blend until pureed. Add cooked squash, maple syrup, salt, and spices. Blend until smooth. Pour into the baked pie crust and chill until set.

Halavah Snacks

1/3 cup raisins

1 cup (firmly packed) grated carrots

1-1/2 cups apple juice

1-1/2 cups brown-rice flour

2 tablespoons mechanically pressed oil

few pinches sea salt

1/3 cup unhulled sesame seeds

1/2 teaspoon non-irradiated cardamom

2/3 cup cooked brown rice

Heat oven to 350 degrees. Oil a square or rectangular cake pan.

Place raisins, carrots, and apple juice in a pot and simmer 5 minutes covered. Remove from heat and let sit 20 minutes.

Place flour in a bowl, add oil, and rub through fingers. Add sea salt and stir with hands.

Drain raisins and carrots and reserve apple juice. Set raisins and carrots aside. Place reserved apple juice in a blender with sesame seeds and cardamom. Blend until smooth. Add blended mixture to flour mixture. Stir well. Add cooked brown rice. Stir. Add raisins and carrots. Mix again.

Pour batter into prepared cake pan. Bake 30 to 40 minutes or until done. Cut into small bars when cooled.

Almond Carrot Oatmeal Cookies

2 cups rolled oats
3-1/2 heaping tablespoons whole-wheat flour or rye flour
1 teaspoon non-irradiated ground cinnamon
1/3 teaspoon sea salt
1/2 cup mechanically pressed corn oil or sesame oil
1/2 cup carrot, peeled and cut into 1/4-inch rounds
2/3 cup ground almonds or pumpkin seeds
1/4 cup barley malt
1/3 cup maple syrup
1/4 cup spring water
1/2 cup raisins

Heat oven to 350 degrees. Oil and flour a cookie sheet.

In a large bowl, place rolled oats, flour, cinnamon, and sea salt. Stir well, then add oil, Rub and sift through hands until crumbly.

In a blender, place carrots, almonds, barley malt, maple syrup, and water. Blend until smooth and no visible carrot pieces remain. Gradually add blended mixture to flour mixture, stirring after each addition. Fold in raisins.

Drop heaping tablespoonsful of batter onto the oiled cookie sheet and flatten with dampened hands. You should have 12 large cookies, about 1/8 inch thick. Bake for 20 minutes or until golden brown. Let cool and remove with a spatula.

The Pumpkin Pie Your Mother Never Gave You (Sunflower Millet Crust)

Sunflower Millet Crust:
- 1/4 cup sunflower seeds, lightly toasted
- 2 cups cooked millet
- 2 pinches sea salt
- 1 tablespoon mechanically pressed oil

Filling:
- 4 cups (or more) kabocha or hokkaido squash, measured after cooking
- 2 cups spring water
- 3 tablespoons agar-agar flakes
- 4 tablespoons rice syrup or maple syrup
- 1 teaspoon non-irradiated cinnamon
- 1/3 teaspoon non-irradiated nutmeg

Prepare crust: Heat oven to 350 degrees. Combine all crust ingredients well with hands. Place in a 9-inch pie pan and press, from the center out and up the sides of the pan, using dampened hands. Bake for 25 minutes and let cool before filling.

To cook squash: Remove seeds from squash and slice into 1-inch cubes. Steam covered in a large frying pan with 2 cups spring water until tender, about 25 minutes. Drain and reserve cooking water. Remove skins from squash if desired.

Place reserved cooking water in a small pot. Sprinkle agar-agar flakes on top of water and let sit 5 minutes. Stir until dissolved. Bring to a boil and simmer 4 minutes, stirring constantly. Remove from heat and add syrup.

Place squash in blender. Add agar-agar mixture, cinnamon, and nutmeg. Blend until smooth. Pour into baked pie shell and let cool in refrigerator 2 hours before serving.

Depression Cake

3/4 cup maple syrup

1/4 cup mirin

1/2 cup mechanically pressed canola oil

1/2 cup raisins

3 teaspoons kuzu, dissolved in 3 tablespoons spring water

2 cups grain coffee (2 cups water and 4 teaspoons grain
    coffee powder)

1 apple, peeled and grated

2-1/2 cups whole-wheat flour

1 cup whole-wheat pastry flour

1-1/2 teaspoons non-irradiated allspice

1 teaspoon non-irradiated cinnamon

1/2 cup walnuts, for garnish

*Based on a recipe
from the Great Depression when people
couldn't afford butter and eggs.*

Heat oven to 350 degrees. Oil and flour a cake pan.

Place maple syrup, mirin, oil, raisins, dissolved kuzu, grain coffee, and apple in a pot. Simmer 10 minutes. Let cool completely.

Combine flour and spices in a large mixing bowl. Add cooked mixture to dry ingredients. Stir very well.

Pour into prepared cake pan. Bake for 55 to 60 minutes, or until done. Press walnuts into top of cake after removing from oven. Let cool.

Romanian Poppyseed Cake

1-1/2 cups soy milk

1/3 cup mechanically pressed canola, sesame, corn, or flaxseed oil

7/8 cup maple syrup

1/2 cup poppy seeds

1/2 teaspoon non-irradiated cinnamon, cardamom, or coriander

1-1/2 cups brown-rice flour

1-1/2 cups whole-wheat flour

1/2 teaspoon sea salt

1/2 cup soy milk

2 teaspoons finely grated lemon peel

juice of 2 lemons

2 tablespoons brown-rice vinegar

I like to punch holes in the cake with a skewer and pour mirin over the top and let the cake absorb it.

Heat oven to 350 degrees. Oil and flour a round or square cake pan.

Place the 1-1/2 cups soy milk, oil, maple syrup, poppy seeds, and spice in a small saucepan. Bring to a simmer and remove from heat. Let cool, or refrigerate to save time.

In a large bowl, combine flours and sea salt. Gradually add cooled mixture, stirring well with a rice paddle after each addition. Add the 1/2 cup soy milk, lemon peel, lemon juice, and vinegar, stirring well.

Pour batter into prepared pan. Bake for 50 minutes or until the center appears the same as the sides. Allow cake to remain in the pan for 3 hours before removing. For the best flavor, let cake stand 24 hours before serving.

CUSTARDS AND PUDDINGS

Indian Pudding
Sourdough Bread Pudding
Apricot Ambrosia
Carrot Halavah
Cappucino Custard (Caramel Sauce)
Carob Amazake Cream
Pumpkin Seed Pudding
Sesame Milk Rice Pudding
Sesame Carrot Custard
Carrot Ginger Creme
Amazake Coffee Gello
Apricot Millet Creme
No-Bake, Near Eastern Rice Pudding
Almond Rice Pudding

Indian Pudding

1/2 cup raisins

spring water

2 cups mashed cooked butternut squash

2 cups cooked cracked-wheat cereal

1 teaspoon mechanically pressed oil

1/2 teaspoon non-irradiated cinnamon

1/2 teaspoon non-irradiated nutmeg

1/2 teaspoon non-irradiated ground ginger

1/2 teaspoon sea salt

5 tablespoons maple syrup or rice syrup

1/8 cup cornmeal

1/4 cup ground pumpkin seeds

Heat oven to 350 degrees. Oil a loaf pan or a round cake pan.

Soak raisins until plump in just enough boiling water to cover.

Combine squash, cereal, oil, spices, salt, and syrup. Mix well. Slowly add cornmeal by sprinkling on top, then stirring. The consistency will be stiff. Add ground seeds and stir. Fold in raisins and any remaining soaking water and stir until evenly distributed.

Place in prepared pan. Cover and bake 45 minutes. Let cool.

Sourdough Bread Pudding

3 cups sourdough bread
1/2 cup sesame or sunflower seeds with 2 cups spring water
1/3 cup maple syrup
1 teaspoon non-irradiated cinnamon
2 handfuls raw sunflower seeds

*Instead of seed milk,
try two cups amazake.*

Heat oven to 325 degrees. Oil a pie plate or small square cake pan.

Thinly slice top crust from bread, if hard. Cube bread to measure 3 cups.

Place 1/2 cup seeds in a blender. Pour in spring water to 1/2 inch above seeds. Blend until seeds are ground. Add remainder of water and blend on high speed another 30 seconds or until an even consistency.

Place bread cubes in large bowl and roll cubes between fingertips to make into crumbs. Add blended seeds (seed milk), stir. Add maple syrup, stir. Add cinnamon and the 2 handfuls of sunflower seeds. Stir again to make sure seeds are evenly distributed through the pudding.

Place in prepared pan. Bake about 50 minutes or until browned.

Apricot Ambrosia

1 cup (very loosely packed) organic dried apricots

2 cups spring water

1/2 teaspoon non-irradiated ground cardamom

1 teaspoon vanilla

1-1/4 cups cooked brown rice

12 whole blanched almonds, for garnish

Simmer dried apricots for 5 minutes, covered, in 1 cup of the water. Remove from heat and let stand 20 minutes.

Place remaining ingredients in a blender with cooked apricots plus cooking water (if any). Blend until mixture is smooth and no longer grainy. Place in serving dish. Garnish with almonds and chill.

Carrot Halavah

3/4 cup raw almonds
3 cups spring water
4 cups carrots, peeled and grated
1/3 cup maple syrup
4 tablespoon mechanically pressed safflower or sesame oil
3 non-irradiated cardamom pods
1/4 cup raisins
1/4 cup raw pumpkin seeds

Place almonds in a blender. Add water to just 1/4 inch above almonds. Blend until almonds are ground. Add remaining water and blend until milky and almonds have almost dissolved. Pour through a fine strainer. (Discard pulp or use in a cake or cookie recipe.)

Combine blended almonds (almond milk), carrots, maple syrup, oil, and cardamom pods in a large saucepan. Bring to a boil. Simmer over low heat, stirring occasionally, until almost all liquid has been absorbed. Add raisins and pumpkin seeds. Continue to cook another 10 to 15 minutes or until all liquid is absorbed. Remove from heat and remove cardamom pods. Pour into serving dish, cover, and let stand 30 minutes.

Cappucino Custard (Caramel Sauce)

3 cups plain soy milk
5 tablespoons (rounded) agar-agar flakes
1/4 cup rice syrup
1/4 cup maple syrup
1/2 cup apple juice
1/2 cup organic carrot juice
5 tablespoons (rounded) grain coffee powder
1/2 tablespoon carob powder, optional
4 tablespoons kuzu, dissolved in 1/2 cup spring water
1/2 tablespoon mechanically pressed canola or corn oil
1/3 cup toasted almonds, chopped, optional garnish

Caramel Sauce:
4 tablespoons barley malt
2 tablespoons maple syrup
1-1/2 tablespoons boiling water
1/2 teaspoon natural vanilla, optional

Instead of carrot juice, you could use one-half cup cooked sliced carrots blended with one-half cup cooking water.

Place soy milk in a medium saucepan. Sprinkle agar-agar flakes on top and stir for a few seconds. Set aside.

In a blender, place rice syrup, maple syrup, apple juice, carrot juice or blended carrots, grain coffee, and carob powder. Stir by hand for 5 seconds. Blend on high speed for 5 seconds. Add blended mixture to soy milk mixture. Stir until evenly combined. Add dissolved kuzu and stir well.

Place saucepan over medium-high heat and bring mixture to a boil, stirring almost constantly with a rice paddle. Turn heat to medium and cook for another 8 minutes, stirring constantly, scraping bottom and sides of pot to prevent kuzu and agar-agar from sticking. Remove from heat and pour into a large ceramic dish or stainless steel pan and let cool for 1 hour. Do not refrigerate. Pour mixture into a blender, add oil and blend on high speed for 45 seconds.

In a bowl, combine caramel sauce ingredients and stir well. Spoon a few tablespoons of sauce into each of 4 individual 8 oz. cups (or 6 to 8 flan-sized cups). Pour custard over caramel. Refrigerate until set; 5 hours or overnight. To serve, run a small knife around the edge of each cup, place a small serving plate on top of cup and turn over. Let set a minute (do not remove cup). Shake cup. Remove cup. Garnish custard with chopped almonds if you want.

Carob Amazake Cream

3 cups plain amazake
1/2 cup apple juice
2 tablespoons carob powder
1 tablespoon grain coffee
1/4 cup rice syrup, optional
1/8 cup maple syrup
1 pinch sea salt
4 tablespoons agar-agar flakes
3 tablespoons kuzu, dissolved in 1/2 cup spring water
1/3 cup toasted almonds, chopped, as garnish

Place all ingredients except agar-agar, kuzu, and almonds in a blender. Blend a few seconds, then pour into a medium saucepan. Sprinkle agar-agar flakes on top and let set for 5 minutes. Add kuzu and stir very well. Bring to a slow boil, stirring constantly. Turn heat to medium and cook another 7 minutes, stirring constantly. Remove from heat and let cool 1 hour.

Return mixture to blender and blend a few seconds on high. Pour into serving bowl or individual dishes and chill for 2-1/2 to 3 hours or until set. Garnish with chopped almonds.

Pumpkin Seed Pudding

1 teaspoon non-irradiated anise seeds
2-1/2 cups spring water
3 cups cooked brown rice
1/3 cup ground pumpkin seeds
1/2 cup maple syrup

Boil anise seeds in the 2-1/2 cups water for 5 minutes. Strain out anise seeds and discard, reserving water. Place cooked brown rice and anise water in a pressure cooker and pressure cook for 30 minutes.

Meanwhile, heat oven to 350 degrees about 15 minutes before baking. Add pumpkin seeds and maple syrup to rice and mix well. Place in oiled baking dish. Bake covered for 35 minutes.

Sesame Milk Rice Pudding

1/4 cup raw unhulled sesame seeds, or 1/4 cup sesame tahini

2-3/4 cups spring water

3 cups cooked short-grain brown rice

1/4 cup rice syrup, or to taste

1/2 cup organic thompson raisins

1/2 teaspoon non-irradiated ground cinnamon

1/4 teaspoon non-irradiated ground ginger

2 pinches sea salt

You could save the sesame pulp to use creatively in sauce or cookies.

Heat oven to 350 degrees.

Place sesame seeds or tahini in a blender. Add 1/2 cup of the water. Blend a few seconds or until seeds are ground. Add remaining water and blend a few seconds more to liquify ground seeds. Pour the resulting sesame milk through a strainer and discard pulp.

Place sesame seed milk in a shallow baking pan. Add remaining ingredients and stir until evenly distributed. Cover pan. Bake for 45 minutes. Remove from oven and let cool a few minutes before serving warm, or chill if desired.

Sesame Carrot Custard

2 cups scraped and sliced carrots, simmered in 1 cup spring
water until tender
1-1/2 cups (firmly packed) cooked short-grain brown rice
1/3 cup plus 2 tablespoons rice syrup
1-3/4 cups spring water
1/4 teaspoon sea salt
1/3 teaspoon non-irradiated cinnamon
3 tablespoons tahini
1 tablespoon kuzu, dissolved in 3 tablespoons water
3 tablespoons agar-agar flakes
1 Sunflower Millet Crust, baked, optional

*This is not too sweet at all.
Add a few tablespoons maple syrup
or more rice syrup if you would
like it sweeter.*

Combine cooked carrots plus cooking water, brown rice, rice syrup,
1-3/4 cups spring water, sea salt, cinnamon, and tahini in a blender.
Blend until creamy.

Pour mixture into a saucepan and add kuzu, stirring well. Sprinkle
agar-agar flakes on top, let set 3 minutes, then stir well. Bring to a boil,
stirring constantly, then turn heat to medium-low and cook 5 minutes,
stirring constantly. Pour into a ceramic bowl and let cool 1 hour at
room temperature.

Return custard to blender and blend 1 minute at high speed. Pour
back into the ceramic bowl or into individual serving cups. Or, if desired, pour into baked pie shell. Refrigerate 3 hours before serving.

✻✻✻✻✻✻✻✻✻✻✻✻✻✻✻
Carrot Ginger Crème ✻
✻✻ ✻ ✻ ✻ ✻ ✻✻✻✻✻✻✻✻✻✻✻

3 cups thinly sliced carrots, simmered until soft in 1/2 cup spring
water
1 cup plain amazake
1/2 teaspoon finely grated ginger
1/2 cup cooked sweet brown rice or short-grain brown rice
1/2 teaspoon grain coffee
2 tablespoons agar-agar flakes

Place cooked carrots plus 1/4 cup of carrot cooking water, amazake,
ginger, sweet brown rice, and grain coffee in a blender. Blend until
smooth and creamy.

Place blended mixture in a saucepan and sprinkle agar-agar flakes
on top. Let sit 5 minutes. Stir flakes in well, then bring to a fast boil,
stirring constantly with a wooden rice paddle. Turn heat to low and let
simmer 3 minutes, stirring constantly. Remove from heat and pour
into a bowl. Let cool 45 minutes.

Return mixture to blender and blend until smooth. Pour into a ceramic bowl or small dessert cups and refrigerate 3 hours or until set.

Amazake Coffee Gello

4 cups plain amazake
2 generous tablespoons kuzu, dissolved in 4 tablespoons spring water
3 tablespoons grain coffee, dissolved in 2 tablespoons spring water
3 tablespoons agar-agar flakes
1/4 teaspoon non-irradiated cinnamon

Place amazake in a saucepan and add kuzu. Stir. Add grain coffee, then sprinkle agar-agar flakes on top and let sit 5 minutes. Add cinnamon and stir well. Bring to a boil and turn down heat to medium-low. Cook for 12 minutes, stirring constantly with a wooden rice paddle. Remove from heat and place in a large bowl. Let cool 1 hour.

Place mixture in a blender and blend until smooth. Pour back into bowl and chill until set.

Apricot Millet Creme

3/4 cup organic dried apricots, chopped

3/4 cup apple juice

1-1/2 cups cooked millet

1-1/2 cups spring water

1/2 cup rice syrup

pinch of non-irradiated cinnamon

1 tablespoon tahini

3/4-inch piece fresh ginger, peeled and finely grated

2 tablespoons kuzu, dissolved in 4 tablespoons spring water

2 tablespoons agar-agar flakes

Place apricots and apple juice in a small saucepan and bring to boil. Turn heat to low and simmer for 5 minutes. Remove from heat, cover, and let stand 1/2 hour.

In a blender place millet, water, rice syrup, cinnamon, tahini, ginger, and apricot mixture. Blend until very smooth and of uniform consistency. Place in a medium saucepan. Add kuzu and stir until combined. Sprinkle agar-agar flakes on top and let set until it dissolves into the mixture.

Place saucepan over medium-high heat and bring mixture to a boil, stirring constantly with a rice paddle. Turn heat to medium-low and cook 5 minutes more, stirring. Let cool 1 hour.

Return mixture to blender and blend a few seconds on high. Pour into dessert cups or serving bowl. Chill 3 hours or until set.

No-Bake, Near Eastern Rice Pudding

6 cups cooked brown rice (preferably basmati)
6 cups spring water
few pinches sea salt
2 cups brown-rice syrup, or 1-1/2 cups maple syrup
1 tablespoon sesame tahini
2 teaspoons non-irradiated ground cardamom
1 teaspoon non-irradiated ground cinnamon
5 tablespoons finely ground brown-rice flour
4 tablespoons kuzu, dissolved in a few tablespoons water
1 cup thompson raisins
1/3 cup crushed toasted almonds or pine nuts, as garnish

*For a sweeter pudding,
replace three of the cups of water
with three cups apple juice.*

Place cooked rice, spring water, and sea salt in a pressure cooker and pressure cook for 40 minutes over low heat with flame deflector. Remove from heat and let sit 1 hour.

Process two-thirds of the pressure-cooked rice through a food mill to produce rice cream. Place the rice cream in a pot and add syrup, tahini, spices, brown-rice flour, and kuzu. Cook over low heat, stirring constantly until mixture thickens. Remove from heat and add the remaining one-third of pressure-cooked rice. Fold in raisins. Pour into a bowl and let cool. Garnish with toasted almonds or pine nuts.

Almond Rice Pudding

2/3 to 3/4 cup short-grain brown rice, uncooked
1/2 cup shelled almonds
4 to 4-1/2 cups spring water
1/3 cup maple syrup plus 1/4 cup mirin, or 1/2 cup mirin plus
    2 tablespoons maple syrup
1/2 teaspoon sea salt
2/3 cup raisins, soaked until plump in hot water to cover, optional
sprinkle of non-irradiated cinnamon, optional

Place brown rice, almonds, and 1 cup of the water in a blender and blend until rice and almonds are finely ground. Add 1/2 cup more water if mixture becomes too stiff to blend. Place blended mixture in a medium-large heavy pot with a lid.

Add maple syrup, mirin, and sea salt, mixing well with a wooden rice paddle. Place pot over a medium flame and gradually add remaining water, stirring constantly until mixture begins to boil. Scrape the bottom and sides of the pot as you stir. Turn flame to very low and cover pot. Let simmer 35 to 40 minutes, stirring occasionally and scraping the bottom and sides of the pot so mixture does not stick. Turn off flame. If desired, add soaked raisins and sprinkle with cinnamon. Cover pot and let sit 30 minutes. Serve warm or chilled.

SEED TREATS, SNACKS, AND MORE
Three-Seed Halavah
Two-Seed Halavah
Sesame Halavah
Brown Rice Sunflower Halavah
Brown Rice Pumpkin Halavah
Seed Squares
Pumpkin Seed Nori Crackers
Crunchy Millet Dinner Squares
Parlor Snacks or Biscuits
Fast Food Dinner Squares
Millet Quinoa Snacks
Millet Sunflower Pizza
Three Grain Millet Piecrust
Flourless Millet Oat Piecrust

Three-Seed Halavah

1/2 cup spring water
1/2 cup organic raisins
1 cup unhulled sesame seeds
1/2 cup sunflower seeds
3/4 cup pumpkin seeds
1/4 teaspoon sea salt

Boil spring water and pour over raisins in small bowl. Set aside.

Roast sesame seeds, sunflower seeds and pumpkin seeds separately in frying pan until they are fragrant and begin to pop. Place roasted seeds in a bowl to cool.

Grind seeds in a blender, about 1 cup at a time. Place in a large bowl. Add salt and mix.

Place raisins with soaking water in blender and puree until smooth. Add blended raisins to seed mixture and mix well. Place in small container and press down evenly. Cover and refrigerate until ready to serve.

Two-Seed Halavah

1 cup unhulled sesame seeds
3/4 cup raw pumpkin seeds
1/4 to 1/2 cup oat flakes or rolled oats
1/3 to 1/2 cup rice syrup
1/4 to 1/3 cup raisins

Try adding one teaspoon diluted barley miso to halavah before placing in small container - mix and knead miso into halavah then press into container.

Roast sesame seeds, pumpkin seeds, and oat flakes separately in a frying pan until aromatic. Place roasted seeds and oats in a large bowl to cool.

Grind seeds and oats in a blender, about 1 cup at a time. Or, grind warm seeds in a suribachi. Place ground seeds and oats in a bowl and add rice syrup. Mix with a wooden spoon. Press into a small container and top with raisins.

Sesame Halavah

1/4 cup rolled oats
1 cup unhulled sesame seeds
rice syrup or barley malt syrup, to taste
1/2 teaspoon fresh ginger juice, or non-irradiated ground
    cinnamon, optional

Grind oats in a blender until a fine powder. Transfer to a bowl and set aside.

Grind sesame seeds in a blender until a meal-like consistency. Transfer to another bowl and add just enough grain syrup to sweeten to your taste and make mixture kneadable. If desired, add ginger juice or cinnamon. Knead. Form into small balls, or into a log, then roll in oat powder.

Brown Rice Sunflower Halavah

1/4 cup raw sunflower seeds, lightly toasted
1/2 cup cooked medium-grain brown rice
1/3 cup organic raisins (thompson or monnukah)
2 tablespoons maple syrup
2 tablespoons quick-cooking rolled oats, toasted
3/4 teaspoon grain-coffee powder
1/2 teaspoon miso

Grind sunflower seeds in a blender. Combine with remaining ingredients and knead into a ball with dampened hands. Form into 3/4-inch balls and refrigerate, or flatten into cookie shapes on an oiled baking sheet and bake at 350 degrees for 15 minutes.

Brown Rice Pumpkin Halavah

1/4 cup pumpkin seeds, lightly toasted

1/2 cup cooked short-grain brown rice

1/8 cup quick-cooking rolled oats, toasted

2 tablespoons rice syrup (or more for a sweeter taste)

1/4 teaspoon miso

These snacks can be eaten as is or baked for a crispier texture.

Grind pumpkin seeds in a blender. Add ground seeds to remaining ingredients in a bowl. Knead into a ball with dampened hands. Form into 3/4-inch balls and refrigerate, or flatten into cookie shapes on an oiled baking sheet and bake at 350 degrees for 15 minutes.

Seed Squares

2-1/2 cups brown-rice flour

1/2 cup sunflower seeds, toasted

2 tablespoons unhulled sesame seeds, toasted

2 tablespoons rolled oats

1/4 teaspoon sea salt

2 tablespoons mechanically pressed sesame or corn oil

2/3 cup organic raisins or currants

1-1/2 cups apple juice

Heat oven to 350 degrees. Oil a lasagna pan or a cookie sheet.

Combine flour, seeds, oats, and sea salt in a large bowl. Add oil and rub mixture between the palms of your hands. Add raisins and mix. Add apple juice and mix well.

Spread dough onto the prepared pan. Form dough into an even rectangle, 1/4-inch thick, pressing down with dampened hands evenly and smoothly. Cut into 8 or 12 squares. Bake for 30 minutes.

Pumpkin Seed Nori Crackers

1-1/4 cups pumpkin seeds, lightly roasted

2 cups brown-rice flour

1 cup boiling spring water

2 tablespoons mirin

3 tablespoons natural soy sayce

1 teaspoon nori flakes

Try substituting dulse powder for nori flakes.

Heat oven to 350 degrees.

Grind pumpkin seeds in a blender or suribachi. Combine ground seeds with brown-rice flour in a large bowl. Gradually add boiling water, mirin, and soy sauce and mix well, then knead for 2 minutes. Add nori flakes and knead for 30 seconds.

Form dough into a ball and place ball in the center of a 9 x 13-inch unoiled pan. Press from the center out, using dampened hands, until dough is evenly distributed in the pan. Cut into 12 squares. Bake approximately 25 minutes. Let cool. Remove from sheet.

Crunchy Millet Dinner Squares

1 cup ground millet (grind millet to fine powder in blender)
1/4 cup ground sunflower seeds
1-1/2 cups rolled oats
1/8 teaspoon sea salt
3 tablespoons mechanically pressed canola oil
3 tablespoons finely grated onion
1-1/2 cups spring water
1/2 cup cooked quinoa or millet

Place ground millet in a large bowl. Add ground sunflower seeds, rolled oats, sea salt, and oil. Mix by rubbing between the palms of your hands. Add onion and water. Mix well with a wooden spoon. Dough will be dense and thick. Cover top of bowl with a plate and let stand 1 hour.

Heat oven to 350 degrees 20 minutes before baking. Oil a 9 x 13-inch pan. Fold cooked grain into dough and mix well. Spread into prepared pan. Dampen hands and pat down to even out. Bake 45 minutes uncovered. Cut into 12 squares and serve warm or cool.

Parlor Snacks or Biscuits

1 cup millet
1 cup quinoa flour
1/3 cup coarsely ground peanuts
1/2 teaspoon sea salt
3/4 teaspoon non-irradiated ground cinnamon
3 tablespoons mechanically pressed canola, sesame, or corn oil
1/2 cup spring water

You can use toasted sunflower seeds in place of peanuts.

Grind millet in blender until powder-fine. Pour into a large bowl and add the quinoa flour, ground peanuts, sea salt, and cinnamon. Add 2 tablespoons oil and rub through the palms of your hands until evenly distributed. Add enough water to form a dough, adding a few more tablespoons of water if needed.

Turn out on a lightly floured board and knead a few times until elastic and of earlobe consistency. Form into a log about 7 inches long and flatten ends. Wrap in plastic or wax paper and refrigerate 1-1/2 hours.

Heat oven to 350 degrees 20 minutes before baking. Oil a baking sheet. Remove chilled dough from refrigerator, unwrap, and slice about 1/4-inch thick, placing each slice onto the prepared baking sheet. You should have about 26 to 28 slices. Brush slices with remaining oil. Bake for 18 minutes. Do not overbake or snacks will be rock-hard and unchewable. Serve warm or cool.

Fast Food Dinner Squares

1/2 cup unhulled sesame seeds
1-1/3 cups spring water
2 tablespoons mechanically pressed oil
1-1/2 cups rolled oats
1/2 cup cornmeal
1/3 teaspoon sea salt

Place seeds, water, and oil in a blender and process until seeds are ground and mixture is smooth.

In a bowl, combine oats, cornmeal, and sea salt. Add blended mixture to oats mixture and mix well.

Spread into an oiled 9 x 13-inch baking pan, using dampened hands to even out. Let set 1/2 hour before baking, if time permits. Heat oven to 350 degrees 20 minutes before baking. Bake for 30 minutes, covered, then for 5 to 10 minutes uncovered. Slice into 12 squares. Let cool 10 minutes or serve immediately.

Millet Quinoa Snacks

1-1/2 cups cooked millet

1 cup quinoa flour

1/4 cup water

2 tablespoons mechanically pressed canola, corn, or sesame oil

1/4 teaspoon sea salt

3/4 teaspoon non-irradiated ground cinnamon

1/3 cup coarsely ground peanuts, optional

Heat oven to 350 degrees. Oil a baking sheet.

Combine all ingredients except peanuts in a large bowl, smoothing out lumps with hands by squeezing through fingers. Add peanuts, if desired, and combine well.

Spread 1/4-inch thick onto the prepared baking sheet, using dampened hands. Bake for 20 minutes. Let cool. Cut into 12 squares with a sharp knife.

Millet Sunflower Pizza

Carrot Puree:

    6 medium carrots, sliced

    1 onion, chopped

    1 small beet, peeled and sliced

    1/4 cup spring water

    2 tablespoons mirin

    2 teaspoons umeboshi vinegar

    1 to 2 teaspoons dark miso, diluted in 1 tablespoon water

Crust:

    2 cups (firmly packed) cooked millet

    1/2 cup sunflower seeds, toasted

    2 tablespoons mechanically pressed canola or sesame oil

    1/3 teaspoon sea salt

    3/4 teaspoon non-irradiated cinnamon, or 1/8 teaspoon non-
       irradiated ginger

For Millet Sunflower Snacks, prepare
the crust only and bake as instructed.

Bring carrots, onion, beet, and water to a boil. Simmer covered until tender. Remove from heat and puree in a blender, processor, or food mill until smooth. Add a small amount of water if too thick. Add mirin, umeboshi vinegar, and miso and puree a few more seconds. Set aside.

Heat oven to 400 degrees. Oil a baking sheet.

Combine millet, sunflower seeds, oil, sea salt, and cinnamon. Press dough approximately 1/4-inch thick onto the prepared baking sheet, patting down with dampened hands. Brown for 8 to 10 minutes. Top with carrot puree and return to oven to heat through. Cut into 9 squares.

Three-Grain Millet Piecrust

3/4 cup millet
1/2 cup cornmeal
1/2 cup rye flour
1/4 teaspoon sea salt
3 tablespoons mechanically pressed corn oil or canola oil
1/2 to 2/3 cup spring water

Heat oven to 350 degrees. Grind whole millet in blender to make flour.

In a frying pan, gently roast millet flour with cornmeal and rye flour until aromatic. Add sea salt. Place in a mixing bowl and add oil, sifting through hands to evenly distribute. Add water and combine. Shape into a smooth ball and knead a few times.

Place ball of dough in the center of a 9-inch pie pan and press from the center out to the sides, using dampened hands, shaping it to fit the pan. Bake for 30 minutes, or until golden. Fill with desired filling.

Flourless Millet Oat Piecrust

1 cup cooked millet
1/4 cup mechanically pressed canola or sesame oil
1/2 cup spring water
1-1/2 to 1-3/4 cups quick-cooking rolled oats
1/4 teaspoon sea salt

You will have some dough left over; enough for two or three medium cookie-shaped crackers. Bake on an oiled cookie sheet along with piecrust, if desired.

Heat oven to 350 degrees.

Place millet, oil, and water in blender and blend until creamy. Set aside.

In a large bowl, place rolled oats and sea salt; stir well. Add blended mixture to rolled oats and knead for 1 minute. Form into a ball and place ball in the center of an unoiled 9-inch pie pan. Press from the center out with dampened hands, sculpting pie dough about 1/4 inch thick to conform to the shape of the pie pan. Prick holes all over crust with fork before baking. Bake for 35 to 45 minutes, depending on crispness desired. Fill with fruit or squash filling.

The End

BIBLIOGRAPHY

Abehsera, Michel. Zen Macrobiotic Cooking. New York: Avon Books, 1968.

Adler, Kief. Beyond the Staff of Life. California: Naturegraph Publishers, Inc., 1976.

Axcell, Claudia, Diana Cooke, and Vikki Kinmont. Simple Foods for the Pack. California: Sierra Club Books, 1986.

Brothwell, Don and Patricia. Food in Antiquity. New York: Frederick A. Praeger, 1969.

Esko, Edward and Wendy. Macrobiotic Cooking for Everyone. Tokyo: Japan Publications, 1980.

The First Macrobiotic Cookbook. California: George Ohsawa Macrobiotic Foundation, 1985.

Jacob, H. E. Six Thousand Years of Bread. Connecticut: Greenwood Press, 1970.

Kushi, Michio. Macrobiotic Home Remedies, edited by Marc Van Cauwenberghe, M.D. Tokyo and New York: Japan Publications, 1985.

Lerman, Andrea Bliss. The Macrobiotic Community Cookbook. New York: Avery Publishing Group, 1989.

McCarty, Meredith. American Macrobiotic Cuisine. New York: Avery Publishing Group, 1996.

Ohsawa, George. Philosophy of Oriental Medicine. Oroville, California: George Ohsawa Macrobiotic Foundation, 1991.

Ohsawa, George. Zen Macrobiotics, Unabridged Edition. Oroville, California: George Ohsawa Macrobiotic Foundation, 1995.

Ray, Sumana. Indian Regional Cooking. New Jersey: Chartwell Books, 1986.

Robertson, Laurel, Carol Flinders, and Bronwen Godfrey. Laurel's Kitchen. New York: Bantam Books, 1976.

Shuman, Sandy. Macrobiotic Desserts. California: Dictionart, 1981.

Tannahill, Reay. Food in History. New York: Crown Publishers, 1989.

Taylor, Colin F., ed. The Native Americans. New York: Smithmark, 1992.

INDEX

142 - VALLEY OF MAIZE

ABOUT THE AUTHOR

Natalie Buckley Rowland grew up in the Bronx, New York, attending Herbert H. Lehman College where she earned her B.A. in Education and Fine Arts, specializing in printmaking.

After graduating she turned to the health-care field, working with the disabled as a Recreation Therapist, using modalities such as art, music, and cooking as therapeutic tools. She went on to study Media and Communications at the New School for Social Research in New York City, returning to the health-care field one year later.

As well as being a natural-foods cook and caterer, she plays acoustic guitar and does crocheted fiber sculpture and illustration.

Other books from the
George Ohsawa Macrobiotic Foundation

Acid and Alkaline - Herman Aihara; 1986; 121 pp; $8.95

Art of Peace - George Ohsawa; 1990; 150 pp; $7.95

As Easy As 1, 2, 3 - Pamela Henkel and Lee Koch; 1990; 176 pp; $6.95

Basic Macrobiotic Cooking - Julia Ferré; 1987; 275 pp; $12.95

Basic Macrobiotics, Revised Edition - Herman Aihara; 1998; 207 pp; $12.95

Cooking with Rachel - Rachel Albert; 1989; 328 pp; $12.95

Essential Ohsawa - George Ohsawa, edited by Carl Ferré; 1994; 238 pp; $12.95

First Macrobiotic Cookbook - G.O.M.F.; 1985; 140 pp; $9.95

Kaleidoscope - Herman Aihara; 1986; 338 pp; $12.95

Macrobiotic Guidebook for Living - George Ohsawa; 1985; 130 pp; $7.95

Macrobiotics: An Invitation to Health and Happiness - George Ohsawa; 1971; 128 pp; $5.95

Macrobiotics: The Way of Healing - George Ohsawa; 1981; 165 pp; $8.95

Natural Healing from Head to Toe - Cornellia and Herman Aihara with Carl Ferré; 1994; 264 pp; $14.95

Naturally Healthy Gourmet - Margaret Lawson with Tom Monte; 1994; 232 pp; $14.95

Order of the Universe - George Ohsawa; 1986; 103 pp; $7.95

Philosophy of Oriental Medicine - George Ohsawa; 1991; 153 pp; $10.95

Pocket Guide to Macrobiotics - Carl Ferré; 1997; 128 pp; $6.95

Zen Macrobiotics, Unabridged Edition - George Ohsawa, edited by Carl Ferré; 1995; 206 pp; $9.95

A complete selection of macrobiotic books is available from the George Ohsawa Macrobiotic Foundation, P.O. Box 426, Oroville, California 95965; (530) 533-7702. Order toll free: **(800) 232-2372.**